To Bonnieanne

P m.c

2011

Peter J. Murray

A catalogue record for this book is available from the British Library.

ISBN: 978-0-9553415-9-5

Typeset in AdobeGaramond by Avon DataSet Ltd, Bidford-on-Avon, Warwickshire

Printed in the UK by CPI Bookmarque, Croydon, CR0 4TD

The paper and board used in this paperback by Mokee Joe Promotions Ltd
are natural recyclable products made from wood grown in sustainable forests.
The manufacturing processes conform to the environmental regulations
of the country of origin.

MJP Ltd
www.peterjmurray.co.uk

Children as young as six years old worked in the textile mills in atrocious and unimaginable conditions.

To those still alive today and those long since gone, this book is dedicated to the memory of them all.

PJM

Prologue

Author Visit

An author came to our school today to give us a talk. He writes scary books – I love scary books. My friends thought it would be boring – but it was brilliant!

He told us how he became an author and then he gave us some tips for writing stories of our own. He said we should look at the people and places around us to get ideas. At the end of the presentation he asked us a question. He asked us what each of us had that would allow us to live out our dreams; enable us to fly like a bird, swim like a fish, go into the deepest dungeons and face unbelievable challenges, such as vampires and werewolves? I put my hand straight up and everyone stared at me.

'Our imagination!' I answered.

I was sat quite near the front. The author looked across at me and smiled.

'Exactly right! Well done!'

My friends looked impressed. I felt really confident and blurted out a question. 'How can I become a writer like you?'

Everyone stared at the author. He asked me my name. I told him I was called Zak.

'I guess you have a wild imagination and you like writing, Zak. Am I right?'

I nodded.

The author smiled again and said, 'Well . . . you're already a writer, Zak . . . just like me.'

My friends gawped at me with their mouths open. I felt really proud. I decided in that moment that I would be a writer for ever.

ZF

Moving In

As soon as Zak saw the house, he felt a bit weird . . . like the house was staring back . . . challenging him to go inside.

He'd no idea why.

It had looked OK in the photographs. His dad had got the house for a bargain price. Everything had happened so quickly and Zak had been at school when his parents had viewed it. So they'd talked to him about it and shown him the 'pics' . . . but this was the first time he'd actually seen it.

The house looked very old – much older than in the brochure. It had a spooky air about it. Zak wondered if it was haunted. And then he chuckled to himself. He *really* did have a wild imagination.

'Dad! How old is it?'

Mr Freeman was getting out of the car after reversing it to make room for the removals van. 'Well . . . I'm not exactly sure. I think it dates back to about 1850. It's as solid as a rock! They don't build 'em like that any more!'

Zak stood to attention in the middle of the road, hands stiffly by his sides, staring across at his new home. He always stood like this when he was concentrating. His friends at school often teased him and called him 'Soldier Boy'.

He gave the house the once-over.

Like all the other houses in the street, it was built of stone – big, grey blocks, mottled with lichens of various shades. There were five windows, three upstairs – one frosted like a bathroom window – and two down. The downstairs windows were crisscrossed with grey strips to give a diamond effect – Zak's mum had said they were 'leaded'.

He craned his neck and stared up at the roof – dark grey slates, many of them covered in green moss – and two chimneys, one at either end.

Mmmm! Maybe there'll be two fireplaces, Zak thought to himself. He loved the open fire at Grandad's house . . . bright dancing flames and the smell of burning wood.

'Dad! Why are there two chimneys?'

Mr Freeman strolled up beside him. He folded his arms across his chest and looked proudly at the front of the house. 'Because the house used to be two cottages. That tall iron gate on the left opens to a passage; if you unlock it you can go through and explore around the back of the house.'

Zak smiled. *Passage . . . this gets better and better!*

The removal men dropped the ramp down at the back of the enormous van with a noisy clatter. Mr Freeman fumbled in his pocket, handed Zak a key and went over to join them.

Zak took the key and shivered a little. It was a dull day – cold and overcast – but at least it wasn't raining . . . not *too* bad for the end of December! He scanned up and down the street. It was deserted . . . just grey terraced houses. He turned and looked at the grim Victorian building behind him. A faded notice board hung on the rusted iron railings edging the playground – 'Steetley Primary School'. Dad had joked about it being a quiet school. The fact was that it had closed down a good few years ago and there was even talk of converting it into flats. Zak wouldn't have gone there in any case. As soon as the holidays were over, he would be joining the year 7's at Airedale High School, about ten minutes away.

He turned back to face the new house. There was just one house to the left of it, a large cat curled up on its stone doorstep – number 25 – and then a dead end, a pathway, or 'snicket' as the locals would refer to it, leading off somewhere.

OK, let's go and have a look down that passage.

He glanced down at the old-fashioned, slightly rusted key in his hand . . . and then across to the iron gate.

But something else caught his eye . . .

The upstairs window of number 25 – the curtains had moved. He looked up, saw nothing, but felt a tinge of nervousness. Convinced there was a half-hidden face peering down at him, he looked away. Walking quickly over to the gate he inserted the key. It turned easily, but the gate refused to move. Zak was big for his age. He pushed hard and it finally jerked open, its hinges creaking and groaning in protest.

Wow!

A narrow passageway paved with cobblestones stretched

out before him. He began to imagine he was Oliver Twist, embarking on some adventure down a London alleyway.

The passage was dark and had a fusty smell. A noise from the far end caught his attention. Someone or something was moving around at the back of the house. 'IS SOMEONE DOWN THERE?' he shouted instinctively.

No one answered.

It was probably one of the removal men . . . *or maybe it was the Artful Dodger!* He chuckled to himself and decided he was being silly.

Taking a deep breath he strode confidently down the passage, his footsteps echoing around the darkened walls. He reached the far end and turned the corner, half expecting someone to be standing there.

There was no one. Just a back yard . . . and lots more cobblestones!

He looked beyond the yard to the garden . . . a simple lawn with flower borders, but no flowers – wrong time of year!

At the bottom of the garden there were *three* sheds!

Now *they* looked interesting! Zak loved garden sheds. They'd had a small one at the last house, but Dad had taken up most of it with his tools. He smiled. Maybe here he could have a shed all to himself. His very own writing den . . . *perfect!*

The noise of a key turning in a lock brought Zak back to his senses. It was the back door to the house.

So many doors!

It opened and his mum smiled at him. 'Hi . . . exploring?'

The sky had grown darker. A thin drizzle began to fall.

'Not really . . . I just came down the passage.'

'Well, it's starting to rain. Why don't you come in and have a look around the house? I bet you're dying to see your room.'

'Mum, has anyone else been out here?'

'Not that I know of! Why?'

'Oh nothing . . . it's just that I thought I heard someone.'

His mum smiled again. Zak recognised the smile. It was the one that said, 'Overactive imagination!' He looked away, slightly embarrassed, and followed her into the house.

*

'Well . . . don't just stand there! Put the light on or you'll break your neck!'

Zak gawped down into the darkness as his dad reached over his shoulder and flicked on the light switch.

Awesome!

A flight of stone steps, coated in flaking red paint, descended before him and disappeared around a corner. A damp, musty smell rose up and filled his nostrils.

A cellar. A real cellar! This gets better and better!

'When you finally pluck up the courage to go down there, be careful! There are some odds and ends lying around. Don't fall over anything.'

'OK, Dad!'

Zak edged slowly down the steps. A draught of cool air rose up from below and caused him to shiver a little. The damp, fusty smell grew stronger.

As he turned the corner, his thoughts turned to castles, dungeons and torture chambers. He could almost hear the agonising screams of prisoners hanging from the ancient stone walls. But, on reaching the bottom step, there was little to see. Just an open space with a low ceiling and lots of dusty wires and pipes overhead.

'Are you OK down there?' Mr Freeman shouted from above.

'Fine, Dad!'

On the left, a long stone table stood against a whitewashed wall. A pile of old newspapers lay skewed across the surface. Zak wondered why the cellar had a stone table.

It must weigh a ton. How did they get that down here?

He walked over and placed the palm of his hand on its smooth surface. It felt cold . . . really cold! The newspapers were fusty and damp. Some of the papers had turned yellow. Underneath the table were some cardboard boxes filled with empty bottles. Zak bent low and took a closer look. The bottles were old and grimy but their labels were still intact. Most were gin bottles, a few of them whisky. There were loads of them.

Zak stepped back, straightened up and suddenly felt an urge to look up . . . and saw the hooks. There were three of them, fixed to the ceiling just above the end of the stone table.

A sudden draught of cold air hit the back of Zak's neck and he spun round. It wasn't easy to see. A dusty lamp bulb draped in spiders' webs gave out little light. It was only then he noticed another doorway.

He began to feel nervous. He crept over to it and peered through. All was in darkness . . . like a black hole! There was another light switch by the door space. He flicked it on.

An eerie glow lit up the small rectangular room.

Zak scanned around.

A pile of logs lay stacked against the right-hand wall. A chopping block lay close to his feet. It had an axe stuck into it. He peered further into the gloom. A heap of black stones were piled up against the far wall. *Coal!* This was the fuel store . . . *no doubt used to supply all those lovely fires.*

He took a few steps into the damp chamber. He felt tense . . . *why?*

A voice called out from above. 'ZAK . . . I'VE MADE YOU A DRINK. DON'T LET IT GO COLD!'

The sound of Mum's voice was reassuring . . . from somewhere back in the world of daylight. Down here, it was gloomy, creepy . . . sinister even . . . and his imagination was starting to get the better of him.

'OK, MUM! COMING!'

He turned and strode towards the main cellar.

And then a sound came from behind . . . like something moving on the coal pile . . . causing lumps of coal to roll down in a small avalanche.

Zak froze.

The disturbance grew louder. All the hairs on Zak's neck stood on end. But he couldn't bring himself to turn round. His body refused to move. Someone was behind him . . . someone big . . . *someone threatening.* He could almost feel the eyes cutting into the back of his head.

Finally, taking a deep breath, he spun round. *He could see nobody . . . nothing!*

And then his body sprang into action.

He sprinted to the bottom of the cellar steps, leapt up them three at a time, reached the top . . . tripped . . . and fell headlong into the kitchen.

2

School's Out

Zak felt a little sad.

It had been OK staying up and seeing in the New Year with his parents: singing Auld Lang Syne to the chimes of Big Ben on TV; eating and drinking more than usual. But Zak would still have preferred a party with lots of people, just as in the last few years. Dad had said that there was too much involved in moving house to have a party. He knew his dad was right, but he would still have preferred one. And now he stood at his bedroom window, staring across at the primary school . . . all closed up, abandoned and deserted. It added to the sad feeling.

He gazed across the empty playground and his mind conjured up images of schoolchildren running around, chasing each other and screaming with excitement. He imagined the teachers striding about amongst them, carrying piles of papers and books under their arms. He could almost see the cars all lined up in the now-empty car park. He could even imagine the dinner ladies with white overalls in the kitchen area, the clatter of pots and pans and the smell of food drifting from the dining room windows.

Zak closed his curtains and lay back on his bed.

'Are you OK?'

He looked round and saw Dad standing in the doorway. 'Fine!'

'Can I come in?'

'Course!'

Mr Freeman walked in and sat on the end of Zak's bed. He was a big man and his weight caused the bedsprings to creak. 'So? A new year and a new start! First impressions? What do you think of the house?'

Zak placed his hands behind his head and smiled. 'I like it. It's pretty big and it's old and there's loads of secret places.'

'Like the cellar with the ghost in it!'

Zak frowned. 'Don't tease, Dad. I nearly had a heart attack down there.'

'And you nearly gave your mum a heart attack when you charged up the cellar steps like that.'

'What do you reckon it was?' Zak asked, looking serious.

His dad folded his arms across his chest. 'A cat!'

Zak shook his head. 'Why would there be a cat down there?'

'You should ask Mum. Apparently, she's been talking to the old lady next door, Mrs Blackham . . .'

'At number 25?' Zak interrupted, thinking back to the movement at the upstairs window.

'Yes . . . she lives on her own. Anyway, she told Mum that the woman who used to live here left her cat behind . . . it wouldn't go with her. It's been hanging around ever since and Mrs Blackham's been feeding it.'

'So how come it's down our cellar?'

'Came in through the coal chute, no doubt. I've been down and had a look round, but there's no sign of it. Probably got out the same way it came in.'

Zak nodded. But he wasn't convinced. The noise had been far too heavy for a cat.

'What about those hooks in the ceiling? What are they for?'

Mr Freeman smiled . . . the knowing smile! 'Well they're not for hanging prisoners on! They were most likely used to hang meat on.'

Zak frowned. That still sounded creepy. His dad saw the look on his face.

'It's my guess that the stone table was used to chop meat and then it was hung on those hooks to keep it cool and fresh. Fridges and freezers haven't been around for ever you know – certainly not when this house was built.'

Mr Freeman got up and put a big hand on Zak's shoulder. Zak liked it when his dad did that – it made him feel safe, secure. 'Now try and get your mind off cellars and stone tables and all that stuff and think about your new school and all the new friends you're going to make. And then try and get some sleep . . . tomorrow there's lots of unpacking to do . . . all sorts of jobs . . . and I *might* have got a nice surprise for you.'

Zak felt a tinge of excitement. 'OK. Goodnight, Dad . . . say goodnight to Mum.'

'Will do!'

Zak crawled under his duvet and pulled the switch cord. The room went really dark, much darker than the bedroom at his last house. Everything seemed so strange here – even the smell of the house, a slightly fusty smell. He closed his eyes and tried to get to sleep, but the radiator over on the wall made a 'clanging' sound. There were other strange sounds too. Zak found himself listening intently, taking them all in. It was ages before he finally dropped off.

*

Zak was dreaming.

In his dream he was standing at his bedroom window, looking down on the playground across the road. It was daylight and the yard was filled with excited children. A group of girls were skipping over by the wall of the main school building. Zak heard their song quite clearly:

> *Scabbajack, Scabbajack*
> *Keep on running . . .*
> *Don't look back*

Still dreaming, he lifted the sash window. Their voices sounded louder:

> *Scabbajack, Scabbajack*
> *He will find you*
> *He will kill you*
> *Sneaky little Scabbajack*

In the real world, Zak tossed and turned.

Back in his dream, he climbed out of his bedroom window, scuttled down the drainpipe and walked over to the playground. Still wearing his pyjamas, he shivered in the chill air, his bare feet felt ice-cold. He gripped the school railings and peered through at the children. Now he could see them clearly. The girls playing the skipping game had white faces, cherry red lips and intense staring eyes. His blood chilled at the sight of them.

They didn't seem to notice him. They carried on skipping and singing . . . their shrill voices ringing in his ears:

> *Scabbajack, Scabbajack*
> *You are never coming back!*

Zak woke up.

He found himself standing at the bedroom window. He thrust back the curtains.

Darkness!

The only light issued from the streetlamp below. The school playground was barely visible, quiet and deserted. He swivelled round. His bedroom was in darkness. The house was still and silent . . . apart from the sound of Dad snoring across the landing.

Zak rubbed his eyes. He looked down at his digital alarm on the bedside table. The red LCD figures stood out clearly:

03.45

He climbed back into bed, turned over and tried to convince himself that he'd just had a bad dream . . . a nightmare. But if it *had* all been nothing more than a nightmare, *why did the soles of his feet feel ice-cold?*

*

Zak attacked his breakfast cereal. He was eager to get out. Lots to do.

'Don't rush your food! You'll get indigestion!'

'Sorry, Mum!' He slowed down a little.

Zak's father frowned at the cardboard boxes scattered around the kitchen floor. He rummaged around in one and spoke to Zak at the same time. 'So what are your plans for today?'

Zak took another spoonful of cereal and spluttered as he spoke. 'More exploring! I think I'll start with the garden.'

'Zak! Don't speak with your mouth full!'

'Sorry, Mum!'

'I suppose you'll be giving the garden sheds the once-over,' Zak's dad said. 'And then you'll be asking me if you can have one all to yourself.'

Zak almost choked on his food. He suddenly remembered the 'surprise'. 'Dad! Can I?'

Mr Freeman chuckled. 'I suppose so. It's not as if I need three sheds. You can have the middle one. It's got power to it and there's a fluorescent light and a wall heater.'

'Brilliant, Dad! Absolutely brilliant!'

Zak's mum smiled. 'I expect you'll want to turn it into a writing den. Somewhere to hide away and let that imagination of yours run riot!'

Zak's dad found his drill in one of the boxes and smiled. 'Sounds good to me! Make the most of it, son. You'll be left school and working before you know it. There's an old textile mill on the other side of the village. I heard it said that kids used to work there from the age of six. Can you believe it?'

Zak's ears pricked up. *Old mill! Sounds interesting!*

Mrs Freeman poured a cup of tea as she spoke. 'Well let's be thankful that those times are past. All Zak needs to think about is his new school. Just another week and then it'll be all systems go.'

Zak smiled to himself. Part of him couldn't wait to get back to school. He missed his English lessons and felt sure that his new school would guide him towards his ambition – to become a real writer one day. He got up from the table, took his cereal dish and spoon and placed them in the sink.

'If you're off down the garden you'll need these,' Zak's dad called to him. He passed Zak a bunch of keys. 'I don't know which one fits which . . . you'll have to try them.'

'Thanks, Dad!' He ran over to the door. 'See you both later.'

'Nobody's doubting that!' Zak's mum teased. 'You'll be back as soon as you're hungry.'

'Watch out for anything sharp!' his dad shouted after him. 'There's all sorts of stuff down there. Take care!'

'OK!'

Zak stepped out of the door into the cobbled back yard.

He looked towards the bottom of the garden. Suddenly, all the nervous feelings and creepy goings-on of yesterday seemed like a distant dream . . . as if they'd never happened. Even his nightmare seemed *like nothing more than a nightmare!*

Today was a new day and the wintry sun was shining and the middle shed looked very impressive.

Yes . . . and it's mine . . . all mine!

With these thoughts racing through his head, Zak charged off down the garden. He never saw his neighbour's curtains move . . . the upstairs back window of number 25. He never saw the little wizened face peeping down at him, the eyes full of curiosity and expectation.

3

Drystone Walls

The three garden sheds stood before him.

He stared at the middle one . . . *his shed!* It was big, rectangular and its longer facing side had a door and a double window. The back of the shed was tight up against a drystone wall bordering the bottom of the garden. The two sheds either side were much smaller and placed at right angles with a single door at one end and a small window in the side. All three sheds were painted dark green and blended well into the garden.

Zak's shed looked the biggest and the best!

He walked up to the door and saw that a big padlock had been slipped through the bolt. He tried several of the keys his dad had given him and soon found the right one. Brimming over with curiosity, he opened the door and stepped inside.

The first thing Zak noticed was the smell – a sort of fusty, oily smell. It was quite pleasant really; it gave the shed an ancient feel. There was an old armchair by the far wall. The chair cover was ripped in a few places and the patterned material seriously faded, but it still looked comfy. Zak walked over and collapsed into it. He sank back into the lumpy upholstery and scanned around his new den.

The walls were decked with shelves, lined with bottles and jars, some empty and some filled with metal objects – nuts and bolts and other odds and ends. One of the bottles was a deep blue colour and Zak recognised it as an old Victorian medicine bottle. His best friend, Charlie Mann, had brought some similar bottles to school when they'd had a Victorian Day.

Zak was about to get out of the chair and go over to the bottle, when . . .

KNOCK!

. . . a sharp rap on the back wall startled him. It wasn't very loud. He wondered if he'd imagined it.

KNOCK . . . KNOCK!

Two raps! Zak tensed. No way had he imagined that! 'WHO IS IT?'

KNOCK . . . KNOCK . . . KNOCK!

Someone was banging on the back of the shed.

Taking a deep breath, Zak rose slowly out of his chair. He crept towards the door.

KNOCK . . . KNOCK . . . KNOCK . . . KNOCK . . . KNOCK . . . KNOCK!

Six loud raps! Zak flung the door open and stepped outside.

There was someone at the back of the shed.

'What are you up to?'

Zak whirled round to see his mum walking towards him.

'What's wrong now?' she asked. 'You look like you've seen a ghost.'

Totally confused, Zak turned towards the drystone wall bordering the back of the shed. He crept down the gap between the sheds and peered around the back . . . no one there! He stretched up and looked over the wall.

And thought he saw something – a shadowy figure maybe – crouching in the dense undergrowth beneath the trees.

'Zak! For Heaven's sake!'

He turned his attention back to his mum. 'I heard someone knocking on the back of the shed. It wasn't you, was it?'

Mrs Freeman smiled. 'Why would I? And if I did, I would hardly knock on the back wall! Let's get inside . . . I've brought you a few things to help you get organised.'

Zak had been so preoccupied with the strange knocking that he'd hardly noticed the bucket of cleaning materials his mum was carrying. She carried the bucket in one hand and a sweeping brush in the other. Zak's dad followed on behind. He was carrying a wad of black bin liners.

'OK!' his dad began. 'While Mum and me are unpacking and sorting things out up at the house, we thought you might like to clean up down here and get your writing den sorted out. And then you can get on with your next bestselling novel!'

Zak forced a smile and nodded thoughtfully. The house, the cellar, the shed, in fact the whole package . . . it was beginning to get to him. He felt sort of excited and frightened at the same time. He decided there was only one thing to do – the thing he loved most . . .

Write about it! So the sooner his writing den was ready, the better!

*

Zak knew that his parents were under a lot of pressure. Back up in the house Dad was desperate to do all the little jobs that needed attention. And Mum was struggling to unpack the countless boxes. The two of them were constantly shifting furniture and trying to work out the best arrangement. On top of all that, Zak's dad was anxious to get to grips with his new building contract. And yet, despite everything, Zak's parents still found time to help and encourage him get his beloved writing den tidy and organised.

Two days it had taken, two hard days of hard work. But now, at last, the shed was clean, dust free . . . and spider free! Zak hated spiders.

Electric sockets were already in place, a convenient one supplying power to Zak's PC, now sitting on the workbench. A trolley with wheels housed his printer and other accessories and his CD player sat on one of the many shelves – Zak liked to have music on in the background, when he was writing: it helped him relax and focus his attention.

He pulled up his leather swivel chair (his most valued possession) and looked at the blank page on the computer screen.

Hmmm . . .

His fingers began typing . . . and then he stopped.

He pushed his seat back and swivelled round . . . looking

over *his* shed for the millionth time. He couldn't quite take it in. It really was all his. Charlie Mann would be so jealous. He swivelled round to face the PC again.

I need to concentrate!

He clicked onto the 'Zak's Journal' file and opened it.

He stretched up to the shelf above his desk and switched on the CD player. As his favourite album began to play, he sank back into his seat, leaned forward and focussed on the keyboard. He took a swig from a glass of fizzy lemonade. After a few more seconds, he began to type:

Moving In

'A new year, a new start,' Dad said, but it's like stepping back in time. The house, the street and the school — everything has a really old feel about it. So far, I've only seen a few people around . . . they looked ancient . . . like from a bygone age. The cobbled passage is a time tunnel! I definitely heard someone at the other end. Who was it? And the noise in the cellar . . . that really freaked me out! No cat ever sounded that loud! I should have had the courage to stay and face it . . . like a superhero! But I'm no superhero . . . just an ordinary boy. And now I will never know. Or will I?

The school across the road gives me the creeps. I wish it wasn't closed down. The deserted playground echoes the silence of the absent children . . . shadows from the past. They already invade my dreams . . . boys and girls with white faces and bright red lips. They sing strange songs about some weird thing called Scabbajack . . . whoever that is.

And finally, the knocking on the back wall of the shed. I'm sure I saw something over the wall . . . hiding in the bushes.

Zak's fingers struck the keys with no errors. He found himself concentrating like never before.

Mysterious forces are at work! I feel excited and scared at the same time . . .

The CD player suddenly stopped. The spell broke and Zak stopped typing. All was silent. He looked around nervously to where the tapping had sounded a few days earlier.

Nothing!

The CD player suddenly restarted . . . a new track. Zak jumped, startled. And then it stopped again.

KNOCK . . . KNOCK . . . KNOCK.

The noise struck terror into Zak's heart. He reacted by standing up abruptly and knocking his drink over. The spillage made a pool on the workbench. He stared down and caught the reflection of his face in the clear liquid, his eyes wide. He moved towards the door . . . stepped out slowly . . . tried to pluck up courage to dart around the back of the shed . . . *Shall I be brave this time . . . a real superhero?*

A strange sort of scraping noise turned his heart to ice. There was definitely someone there, shuffling around.

Zak fled up the garden and disappeared into the house.

4

A Friend in Need

'Are you OK, son? You're very quiet this morning.'

Zak crunched on his cereal and spoke at the same time. 'I'm fine, Dad. Just thinking.'

Mr Freeman looked across at his wife. 'Too much thinking. He needs to get out and get some fresh air.'

Mrs Freeman nodded. 'It's just as well Charlie's coming round to visit. His mum's going to give me a hand hanging some new curtains.'

Zak took another spoonful of Crunchie Munch and frowned. 'Do you two mind! You're talking like I'm not here. I'm not a baby.'

'Oooohhh . . . Get him!' Mr Freeman smiled. 'Touchy, these writer types. What time are they due?'

Mrs Freeman went over to the worktop and put some toast on. 'They should be here any time now.'

'And is it still OK for Charlie to stay over?' Zak asked enthusiastically.

Mrs Freeman nodded. 'Kath's going to pick him up tomorrow lunchtime.'

Zak smiled into his cereal. 'I can't wait to show him around.'

Mrs Freeman brought some lightly buttered toast over and put it on Zak's plate. She looked down at him. 'Zak . . . you look pale. I haven't seen you smile much recently. You do like it here, don't you?'

Silence fell over the kitchen. Mr Freeman, who was about to make a call on his mobile, stopped and looked up.

''S OK!'

'Just OK?' Zak's dad muttered.

'It's quiet.'

'What's quiet?'

Zak stopped eating. He stared vacantly into space. 'Everywhere! The house . . . the garden . . . Even the street seems dead. I've hardly seen anyone.'

Mr Freeman stared at Zak, and then looked across at his wife again.

She nodded solemnly. 'He's right! It is very quiet around here. I've hardly seen a soul since we moved in. I've had one brief chat with the old lady next door and that's about it.'

Mr Freeman frowned and put his mobile down.

'Who lives in the house down from us?' Zak asked.

'Nobody,' his father replied. 'The estate agent said it's been empty for over a year. This one was empty for six months.

That's why we got the house at a knockdown price.'

'What about the rest of the street?'

Mr Freeman looked thoughtful. 'Some of the houses are empty. The area's been a bit depressed for some time . . . ever since the mill closed down. But the general opinion is that things will soon be on the up. The city's doing well and more and more people are moving into the suburbs. Things can only get better for Steetley, believe me.'

'And especially for builders like your dad,' Zak's mum added. 'It's the reason we moved here and I hope we won't regret it.'

Mr Freeman picked up his mobile again and winked at Zak. 'We won't! I've got a lot of work lined up already – and I *don't* mean the work that your mum wants me to do around the house.'

Zak looked back at his father's rugged features. He was smiling, but the frown lines on his forehead told Zak that it was a forced smile. Zak sensed that his dad felt just as uneasy as he did!

A knock sounded from somewhere at the front of the house.

'That must be Kath and Charlie,' Zak's mum said. 'I'll go and let them in.'

Zak watched excitedly as she headed towards the sitting room and on to the front door. She reappeared a few seconds later followed by Kath and Charlie.

Zak beamed as his best friend's cheery features came into view: big white teeth, freckled face, energetic eyes piercing through his gold-rimmed specs, all topped with a head of bushy red hair.

'Hi, Zak . . . What's new?'

Zak felt his spirit begin to lift. 'Nothing much . . .'

Mr Freeman had just finished a phone call. He slipped the mobile in the pocket of his overalls and laughed. 'No – nothing much, Charlie . . . new house, new bedroom, new writing den . . . and maybe a few spooks here and there! Nothing much really!'

Zak pretended he hadn't heard. 'Come on, Charlie. I'll show you my new den.'

Zak's mum put the kettle on and invited Kath to sit at the table. The boys made a quick exit and headed off down the garden.

'There they go . . .' Zak's dad shouted after them. 'THE REAL GHOSTBUSTERS!'

*

Charlie reclined back in the old armchair. Zak sat opposite, swivelling in his leather chair.

'So what's your dad going on about?' Charlie asked.

Zak frowned. 'You mean the Ghostbuster business?'

'Exactly!'

'How long have you got?'

Charlie smiled. Charlie always smiled – he was the most cheerful person Zak had ever met. Unlike Zak, Charlie was small for his age, thin and wiry, but he was rarely scared of anything (or anyone) and nothing ever seemed to upset him. 'You don't really believe in ghosts . . . do you?'

'Well, I didn't! But . . . I'm not sure now. This place is weird.'

Charlie got up, walked over to the window and stared up the garden. 'You mean the house?'

Zak swivelled round to face the same way. 'Not just the house, the whole place – the street, the school across the road . . . everywhere.'

'You sure it's not just that imagination of yours working overtime?'

'Now you're beginning to sound like Mum and Dad! It's *not* just my imagination . . . and I'll prove it.'

'How?'

Zak got out of his chair and headed towards the shed door. 'I'll give you a guided tour. And then you'll see.'

Charlie followed. 'Sounds good to me.'

As the two friends set off up the garden, neither of them saw the small shadowy figure peeping at them from behind the shed . . . crouching . . . shaking . . . desperate to make contact . . . watching their every move.

*

Zak took Charlie to the end of the street, where it met the main road at some traffic lights. The road was busy. They walked up to the safety barrier by the side of the crossing. Charlie leaned on the metal rail. Zak stood to attention, arms by his sides, watching the traffic whizzing past.

'This road is so busy,' Zak commented.

Charlie shrugged his shoulders. 'Course it is, Soldier Boy, it's the main road into the city.'

Zak turned round, rested his back on the barrier and stared back up School Street. 'OK . . . now look up there!'

Charlie followed Zak's gaze. School Street was almost deserted – just a few parked cars and no signs of life. 'Mmmm . . . see what you mean.'

Leaving the roar of the traffic behind, Zak headed back up School Street, beckoning Charlie to follow. As they walked past the terraced houses, Zak made a mental note of which windows had curtains and which didn't . . . most didn't! A few of the houses had 'For Sale' or 'To Let' signs standing outside.

'Blimey!' Charlie exclaimed. 'What a dump! Loads of these houses are empty.'

Zak strode on, taking big determined strides, leaving his friend some distance behind. 'Exactly!' he shouted over his shoulder. 'It's like a ghost town . . . or at least a ghost *street*, anyway.'

They reached the primary school. Zak grasped two of the railings and peered through at the empty playground. He told Charlie about his strange dream – about the weird pupils with the white faces and the bright red lips.

Charlie frowned for the first time. 'Wow! That is one weird dream. They sound like zombies. It gives me the creeps.'

Zak nodded. He gripped the railings more tightly. 'Me too! I can't stop thinking about them.'

Charlie stood at the railings beside Zak. 'This school looks so spooky.'

Zak nodded. 'Mum says it closed a few years ago. Not enough kids!'

'Oh well,' Charlie smiled, 'the kids might be back one day. And then the school won't look so spooky and you won't have any more bad dreams.'

Zak nodded again. 'Come on! I'm going to show you the house . . . and the cellar.'

As they walked across the road, Zak glanced up at the

neighbour's bedroom window. His heart skipped a beat. There was a face there . . . the staring wrinkled face of an old woman. She stared down with piercing eyes, watching their every move.

Charlie glanced up too. He spoke quietly, almost in a whisper. 'Blimey! Who's that?'

Zak grabbed Charlie's arm and marched him over to the passage. 'I think it's our neighbour.'

'Don't like the look of her,' Charlie muttered. 'She's got a face like a witch.'

Zak pushed the iron gate open and pointed down the passageway. 'There was someone down there . . . moving around at the back of the house.'

'When?' Charlie asked, staring down at the cobbles.

'The day we moved in. I heard them.'

'Probably your mum or maybe one of the removal men.'

Zak shook his head. 'I checked.'

The two boys clattered on down the passage and out into the cobbled yard at the back of the house. They sat on a bench by two flower tubs.

Charlie removed his glasses and wiped them on some tissue. He looked up at Zak with big brown eyes and an even bigger grin. 'Mmm . . . you definitely seem hung up about this place. Admitted it's a bit on the quiet side. And that woman next door looks spooky enough. But you've not really shown me anything to get seriously stressed about.'

'OK!' Zak said, determination in his voice. 'Follow me . . . we're going down the cellar.'

He led Charlie into the house, through the kitchen and over to the cellar door. It was slightly open and the light was on. Zak found himself breathing heavily. He opened the door fully and shouted down the cellar steps. 'ANYONE DOWN THERE?'

No answer!

He stepped back into the kitchen. He could hear his mum upstairs talking to Charlie's mum. No doubt they were busy hanging curtains. He shouted upstairs. 'MUM! WE'RE JUST GOING DOWN THE CELLAR.'

Mrs Freeman's voice sounded from somewhere above. 'OK. But be careful down there!'

The two of them started down the steep stone steps. Still wondering why the light was on, Zak shouted ahead again, 'DAD . . . ARE YOU DOWN THERE?'

Still no answer.

'Cellars are so spooky,' Charlie whispered from behind.

'Especially this one,' Zak whispered back. Creeping down a few more steps, the damp musty smell invaded his nostrils. His mind went back to the noise on the coal pile. He was glad that Charlie was with him.

The two friends crept down to the bottom of the steps . . . and turned the corner.

Zak eyes went straight to the stone table . . . and the pool of blood oozing across the surface beneath the hooks. At the same time, a large shadowy figure moved out from the fuel store.

Zak screamed and leapt backwards. Charlie yelled out. They turned and fell over each other . . . ending up in a tangle on the cold stone floor.

5

Sleepover Scares

'You should have seen your faces,' Zak's dad laughed. 'Sheer terror!'

'It's not funny!' Zak retorted. 'You almost gave us a heart attack.'

'We thought it was real blood!' Charlie added, dusting his trackie bottoms down.

Mr Freeman carried a paint can over to the stone table. He began cleaning up the pool of red liquid, salvaging what he could into the tin. 'Red floor paint! That's all it is. I'm free till this afternoon so I decided to give the cellar steps a fresh coat. Unfortunately, I knocked the tin over.'

'So why were you in the fuel store?' Zak asked, annoyance still in his voice.

Mr Freeman smiled to himself. 'Because I heard the two Ghostbusters coming down the steps and I thought I'd give them a scare. And judging by your reaction, I think I succeeded. Don't you?' He laughed out loud again, and Zak gave Charlie a look that said 'Parents can be really annoying, can't they?' Charlie recognised the look and nodded gravely.

By the time the two friends had finished dusting themselves down, Zak was thankful that his heartbeat had returned to normal. He took Charlie into the fuel store, showed him the coal pile and told him in detail about his spooky experience. Mr Freeman continued to mop up the paint spillage and interrupted Zak several times, still insisting that a cat was the most likely explanation and that the rest was in Zak's imagination . . . as usual!

'Never mind him!' Zak whispered. 'I'm telling you, whatever it was it was no cat . . . unless it had boots on! Anyway, I was out of here . . . like lightning! I ran up the cellar steps so fast I nearly killed myself!'

Charlie's big eyes blinked behind his spectacles – he looked convinced!

As Zak turned to leave the fuel store he glanced towards the stone table.

A huge figure stood in his father's place with its back turned towards him. Zak gawped at the sight of the balding head glistening with perspiration, the thick neck, the broad shoulders and muscular arms. It was wearing some kind of apron, tied at the back.

As Zak's mind reeled in confusion, the big man raised a cleaver above his head and brought it down with incredible force onto the stone table. There was a strong smell of meat . . . raw meat . . . and blood!

Zak shrieked, closed his eyes and put a hand to his mouth – he felt sick. His mind refused to believe what he was seeing . . . smelling.

'*Now* what's the matter?' Mr Freeman asked in surprise.

Zak opened his eyes. His dad was standing at the table, brushing what was left of the red paint into the tin.

Charlie nudged his arm. 'Are you all right?' he asked with a look of half concern and half amusement.

Zak shook his head and stuttered. 'Over . . . over . . . there! Disgusting!' He pointed to where his father was standing.

'Well! Thank you very much,' Mr Freeman said, his eyebrows knitted into a puzzled frown.

'Let's get out of here!' Zak said in a determined voice.

'Suits me!' Charlie replied, managing a grin.

The two boys leapt up the cellar steps, Mr Freeman calling after them. 'Take my advice and give up the Ghostbusters routine. You need to take some time out and chill!'

Back in the kitchen, Zak helped himself to a glass of orange juice from the fridge. He took a big swig and then poured one for Charlie. 'Here, get this down,' he ordered his friend. 'I'll ask Mum if we can get the bus into town. Dad's right, we need to get away and chill.'

Charlie sipped from his glass and nodded. 'Sure! But what was all that about?'

'There was a huge man in the cellar, standing at the stone table. I saw him . . . chopping meat. I could even smell the blood. And then he vanished into thin air.'

'But I was there and I didn't see anyone.'

Zak looked straight into Charlie's eyes. 'I'm telling you, I saw him! He looked like a butcher . . . wearing an apron.'

Charlie's eyes gleamed behind his glasses. 'This is so cool! It's like being in a scary movie.'

'Except this is no movie.' Zak sighed.

Mrs Freeman walked into the kitchen. Zak told her his plan, about going into town. She thought it was a great idea. She said it would be good for them to go somewhere a bit more lively, away from Steetley. She gave the boys some money and asked Zak to bring back a couple of items for the evening meal. Charlie's mum got her purse and insisted on giving them their bus fares. A short while later, the boys set off down School Street heading for the bus stop, both mums waving them on their way.

*

Zak lay back in his bed with his hands behind his head. Charlie lay on the camp bed beside him.

The trip to town had been a great success.

As soon as he and Charlie had boarded the 251 to the City, the strange feelings clogging Zak's mind had quickly disappeared. The bus was almost full – young people, old people, families with small children . . . *noise and normality!* And once they were in the city, Steetley seemed a million miles away.

The bright sunny afternoon had brought everyone out. The streets were heaving and Zak and Charlie had thoroughly enjoyed touring the shops, surveying all the CDs, DVDs and the latest computer games. After a couple of hours, their legs had ached and they'd collapsed into a café. Charlie had bought them both a milkshake. The cool drinks had slid down their dry throats – dry from chatting. Zak had told Charlie what he knew about his new school and they'd talked about their old school. They promised each other they would keep in touch by e-mail and send progress reports. After the café, they had walked around the indoor market and come across a stall selling old Action Comics. Charlie had spotted an issue of Superman he'd been after for ages – he bought it for a good price and it had made his day.

All in all it had been a great afternoon and never once did either of the two friends mention the strange incident in the cellar. Neither did they mention Zak's weird dreams or any of the other spooky goings-on around 21 School Street. Suddenly, to Zak, it had all seemed like a distant dream . . . like none of it had ever happened. On the return bus journey Zak had felt more relaxed and more cheerful than he'd done for a long time . . . until they'd arrived back in Steetley.

As soon as Zak had stepped off the bus, the feeling of impending doom had returned. It was like some big black cloud hanging over the street – Charlie had admitted feeling it too.

Well, at least now they were tucked up in bed and Zak wasn't alone.

Charlie grinned his big toothy smile. 'It was good this afternoon, wasn't it?'

Zak nodded and smiled. 'You should have seen your face when you saw that Superman magazine. It was like you'd won the Lottery.'

'It was better than winning the Lottery.' Charlie beamed. 'I don't think that guy knew how rare it was . . . and it's in mint condition.'

'OFF TO SLEEP, YOU TWO!' a familiar voice shouted from downstairs. 'IT'S AFTER TEN!'

'OK, DAD!' Zak called back.

'GOODNIGHT, MR FREEMAN!' Charlie called after him.

'GOODNIGHT . . . SLEEP TIGHT!' Mr Freeman called up.

'See you in the morning,' Charlie said quietly as he snuggled onto his side. 'Let's hope you don't have any of those weird dreams tonight.'

'Yep . . . goodnight!' Zak replied, turning out the light. He focussed his mind on the afternoon's events and drifted off to sleep.

*

Everything was in darkness when Zak woke up . . . that's if he was awake. He wasn't quite sure whether he was dreaming again. His eyes went over to the curtains – a faint chink of streetlight shone through a narrow gap. Butterflies invaded his stomach. He switched on the bedside lamp, got out of bed and crept over to the window.

It's cold, really cold . . . so I can't be dreaming. You don't feel cold when you're dreaming.

He reached out and took hold of the curtains, one in each hand.

They feel real . . . I can't be dreaming.

Taking a deep breath, he drew the curtains back a little and peered out of the window. His heart missed a beat as he saw a small figure standing alone in the centre of the playground.

I am dreaming . . . no one would be standing there at this time of night.

An icy shiver ran down his spine as he realised the figure was looking up at him. It looked like a small boy wearing a big cap. He was standing almost to attention, like Zak sometimes did, arms by his sides, his head angled slightly upwards.

'Charlie, come and look at this!' Zak cried over his shoulder to his sleeping friend.

Charlie mumbled something, turned over and started snoring.

Zak turned back to the window and almost screamed. The figure had moved much closer, across to the edge of the playground, up to the railings, right opposite his window. Though still in shadow, Zak saw the figure much more clearly.

The head looked almost too big for the slim, short body, the shoulders were very narrow. He could see the outline of what looked like a jacket, a scarf tucked in at the neck . . . and ragged trousers to just below the knee. It was definitely a boy, but so old-fashioned looking.

The shadowy figure stood as still as a statue, gripping the iron railings and staring up at Zak's window.

Why is he staring at me?

Zak panicked. He drew the curtains firmly shut and leapt back into bed.

'Charlie . . . Charlie . . .' Zak whispered as loud as he dared.

But Charlie snored even louder.

Zak dared himself to have one last look. He knew he would

never get back to sleep, thinking about that figure out there. He crept back over to the window and peeped out. The figure had disappeared.

This is definitely a dream! I'll just get back in bed and go to sleep and everything will be fine in the morning.

He climbed back into bed again – let his head sink into the pillow. He closed his eyes and tried to clear his mind. And just when he thought he'd succeeded, he had the most awful feeling . . . *that the boy was down in the hallway standing at the bottom of the stairs.* There were no sounds, no front door opening or anything like that, but Zak sensed that something was in the house.

He dived under the duvet, hiding in the blackness. He imagined the ghostly form drifting slowly up the stairs, heading towards his bedroom. An ice-cold shiver ran down his spine again.

This is not happening! It can't be!

He dared himself to peep out from beneath the duvet. He knew he had to do it. This time there was nowhere to run. Taking a deep breath, he edged the duvet down to nose-level and peered over it towards the bottom of the bed.

No one there!

And then he looked towards the landing and saw the pale white face staring in at him.

6

The Widow Blackham

Zak dived back under the duvet into the blackness, blotting out the awful vision and praying that it would go away. After a few seconds, which seemed like an eternity, he took a deep breath and peeped out again.

The ghostly figure was still there.

He stared in horror as it moved silently into the room: slim . . . weedy . . . big head . . . big cap . . . narrow shoulders . . . the same figure he'd seen in the school playground.

'Please go away!' Zak uttered through clenched teeth.

But the figure drifted closer. It stopped at the foot of Zak's bed and stood there, rooted to the spot. Now Zak saw the boy's face in vivid detail. It was unbelievably pale . . . almost white with bright red lips. But the eyes were the worst. Big mournful eyes . . . a sinister mix of sadness and terror. They cut into Zak like a knife and chilled him to the bone.

Zak gulped and took another breath. 'You . . . you're not real! I'm dreaming.' He closed his eyes . . . opened them again. The face stared back even more intensely; its mouth opening wide as if it was trying to say something . . . but no sound came out.

'Go away!' Zak gasped. *'You're not real!'*

The figure began to shake . . . shimmer . . . the eyes growing even bigger. Zak saw the desperation in the face . . . pleading . . . begging. The mouth moved frantically again. What was it trying to say?

Zak closed his eyes and shouted loudly, 'CHARLIE!'

'Whassup?'

At last! Charlie finally stirred. Zak glared at his friend and pointed at the ghostly figure.

Charlie sat up and rubbed his eyes. 'Whassup?' he repeated.

Zak looked back to the end of his bed.

Nothing!

The ghost-boy had completely disappeared! 'I don't believe it!' he muttered under his breath.

Charlie sat up and put his glasses on. Zak got out of bed and walked slowly around the room, checking the dark corners and other possible hiding places. He even checked under the bed.

Nothing!

He crept slowly out onto the landing. The sound of Dad snoring from the big bedroom reassured him. He leaned over the banister and peered downstairs into the hallway, much of it in shadow, but definitely nothing . . . *or nobody* . . . there!

'What's going on?' Charlie called from the bedroom.

Zak's heartbeat slowed down a little. The cold sweat stopped. He got back into bed. But he knew he would never get back to sleep. He looked at the bedside clock. 3.30 a.m.

Charlie sat there looking puzzled. For once he wasn't smiling. His expression was one of genuine concern. 'Are you going to tell me what this is all about or what?'

And so Zak told him in detail everything that had just happened.

At the end of it all, Charlie's eyes had grown so big behind his glasses they reminded Zak of two golf balls.

'And before you ask, it was no dream!' Zak said sternly.

'OK! If you say so!'

'I do say so! It was the scariest thing I've ever seen in my life. But you know what?'

'What?' Charlie gasped.

'It was like that ghost-boy was trying to tell me something . . . like he needs my help.'

Charlie nodded and lay back down. He took his glasses off and put them back in the soft leather case, placing it on the floor by the camp bed. 'But why would he need your help?'

Zak was wondering the same thing. He lay back and stared up at the ceiling.

There was such horror in that boy's face. Those eyes . . . filled with terror. Why?

'I don't know,' Zak sighed. 'But I've got a feeling I'm going to find out.'

Charlie sat up again. 'I think if I saw a ghost I'd be out of here. There's no way . . .'

'I know!' Zak interrupted. 'But I'm beginning to think that all this spooky stuff is happening for a reason.'

Charlie stared at him with a look of awe.

Zak laid his head back on his pillow and glanced at the clock again. 4 a.m.

Charlie saw him looking. 'Suppose we'd better try and get back to sleep. At least it'll soon be morning.'

'Not soon enough!' Zak said seriously. He turned over, reached out to switch off his bedside lamp . . . and changed his mind. *He decided he would rather leave the light on!*

*

Zak's mum prepared the boys an excellent fried breakfast – eggs, bacon, tomatoes, sausages and fried bread. Zak and Charlie ate the lot.

'You two were hungry!' Zak's mum smiled.

'Too true!' Zak's dad added. 'Waste-disposal units – that's what you two are!'

Zak took a slurp from his mug of tea. 'Can't hang about! Things to do!'

'Like what?' Mrs Freeman asked with raised eyebrows.

Charlie beamed at her, 'Ghost hunting!'

Mr Freeman slipped his jacket on and picked up his car keys. He cracked out laughing. 'Well, well! The Real Ghostbusters are still in business! And where are you going to start this time? Don't tell me . . . down the cellar?'

Zak felt his face flush with embarrassment. 'No, we're not! And in any case, we're not really ghost hunting. We're just going outside to nose around a bit. We want to find out why everything's so quiet and mysterious around these parts.'

Mrs Freeman plunged a hot pan into a washing-up bowl. The pan hissed like a snake. 'You just be careful. Nosing around can land people in serious trouble.'

Zak nodded and got up from the table. Charlie did the same.

'And before you go off and start your investigations, you can drop this letter off at the neighbour's house. The postman pushed it through our letter box by mistake.'

Zak felt a knot form in his stomach. 'You mean the old . . .' He was about to say 'witch', but managed to stop himself. 'The old woman at number 25?'

Zak's mum nodded. 'Mrs Blackham! That's her name. She seems a lonely old soul. Why don't you knock on the door, give her the letter and say who you are? I think she'd appreciate that.'

Zak took the brown envelope from his mum; it looked like a bill. 'OK, Mum! We'll see to it.'

'And make sure you're back by lunchtime. Charlie, your mum will be here to collect you at two.'

'Fine, Mrs Freeman.' Charlie smiled. 'We'll be back. See you later.'

'Don't forget your ghostbusting lasers!' Mr Freeman chortled. 'You never know when you might need them!'

Zak looked at Charlie and frowned . . . and then the two of them disappeared hastily out through the back door.

A blast of cold air greeted them. It was bright and sunny, but freezing cold. They marched down the passage, turned up the street and faced the weathered door of number 25. Zak was about to knock when a loud rapping sound startled him. He and Charlie looked to their left and saw the old wrinkled face staring at them through the sitting room window. She was tapping on the glass.

'It's her . . . the old witch!' Charlie uttered. 'I think she's trying to say something.'

Zak strained his ears, but he couldn't quite hear what she was saying. And then the face disappeared.

'Quick! Let's go!' Charlie exclaimed. 'That woman gives me the creeps.'

Zak was in agreement. He decided to thrust the envelope through the letter box and make a run for it . . . but then he had another idea. He turned to Charlie. 'She might know something!'

Before anyone could say anything else, the door opened and the old lady was standing there. She wrung her hands together and looked up at them. Small and twisted, she reminded Zak of a gnarled old tree.

'Don't just stand there!' she said in a shaky old voice. 'Come in . . . and bring that letter with you. I suppose it's mine. That postman gets worse. I'll swing for him one of these days.'

Zak and Charlie followed her down the hallway; it had a musty smell. The wallpaper was a faded yellowy-brown – some sort of flowery pattern, peeling in places. They passed a couple of closed doors. Zak wondered what might be hiding behind them.

'Bring it into the kitchen and sit down. I'd like a word.'

The kitchen was a disaster. The untidiest room Zak had ever seen. An ancient wooden table was covered in plates, cups and various items of food: mainly biscuits, bread and jars of marmalade and jam with no lids. One of the jars lay on its side and some sticky liquid had spilled out onto the plastic tablecloth. There were crumbs everywhere!

Zak pulled a stool from under the table – it felt greasy. He sat on it, somewhat reluctantly. Charlie sat on a grubby-looking chair opposite. The old woman stood with her back to the sink, her arms folded across her chest, staring into Zak's eyes.

'You're just like him,' she said almost accusingly.

Zak felt his mouth began to dry up. 'Like who?'

'Jack.'

Charlie turned to face her. 'Who's Jack?'

The old woman's eyes misted over. Tears formed in her eyes as she continued to gaze at Zak. 'Our Jack . . . Jack Craddock.'

'Who's Jack Cra . . .?' Charlie started.

'You've seen him, haven't you?' she interrupted, her voice full of concern.

Zak took a deep breath. 'Look, Mrs . . .'

She cut in again, 'Most of the folk around here call me "The Widow Blackham". You can call me Mrs B.'

Zak relaxed a little. 'Who's Jack Craddock?'

Mrs B walked over to the table, pulled out another chair and sat down between the two boys. She pushed a dirty plate to one side, folded her arms on the table and stared into space.

'Jack Craddock is a poor soul searching for justice.'

Zak's stomach tightened. He stared at Charlie. Charlie stared back – he wasn't smiling.

Mrs B turned to Zak again. 'Like I said . . . you've seen him, haven't you? And that house of yours . . . you know it's haunted?'

Zak gulped. His mind went blank.

It was Charlie who asked the next question: 'And who's supposed to be haunting it?'

The old woman suddenly stiffened, her eyes shifting rapidly from one boy to the other. 'The butcher . . . the baker . . . the candlestick maker!' She began to cackle like a witch.

Zak wondered if Mrs B was completely mad. By the look on Charlie's face, he was thinking the same thing.

Mrs B leaned forward so that her face was only inches away from Zak's. He could smell her stale breath. She looked deep into his eyes. 'Everything comes right with time. What goes around comes around. Our Jack deserves justice and you'll see to it!'

Zak was dumbfounded. Mrs B was *definitely* mad . . . surely the mutterings of a lonely old woman . . . *and yet?*

'Just tell me. You have seen him, haven't you?' she pleaded. 'The boy with the big eyes!'

Zak suddenly saw the desperation in her face. He began to feel sorry for her. He nodded slowly. 'Well . . . I think I've seen him!'

Mrs B slumped onto the table, sending a dirty spoon and a tea-stained saucer crashing onto the floor. 'May the Saints preserve us! I knew it!'

Zak's head was in a spin. He began to feel faint. He stood up and headed towards the door. Charlie followed his example.

Mrs B dragged herself up onto her elbows and shouted after them. 'I'm sorry! I didn't mean to frighten you. Jack's a tormented soul, but he won't hurt you. He never did anyone any harm.'

'Got to go,' Zak shouted over his shoulder. 'Your letter's on the table.'

The old lady struggled to her feet. 'If you don't want to talk to me . . . talk to The Ferret.'

Charlie called back. 'Who's The Ferret?'

Mrs B struggled after them down the fusty hallway. 'He's the security man at Greenlands . . . where all the trouble started. He'll tell you about Jack.'

Zak's head was still reeling. He needed to get out, back into the fresh air. The fusty smell, the gloom and the weird happenings were just too much! Charlie scurried after him. They struggled to open the door – it was sticking.

'Where will we find The Ferret?' Charlie asked.

Mrs B cackled like a witch again. 'Like I said, he's down at Greenlands. Get yourselves down there and he'll find you soon enough. Or at least Rufus will!'

'Right . . . thanks!' Zak spluttered, finally opening the door wide enough to squeeze through.

'See you!' Charlie added, following behind.

Mrs B stood in the doorway shouting after them. 'That cat . . . he'll tell you when something's afoot. Keep him close!'

The door slammed behind them. They quickly moved away. From the far side of the road Zak looked back to the old woman's front window . . . almost certain of what he would see. At first there was no one there, but a moment later the old wrinkled face was back, staring out with hollowed eyes. She was pointing behind him.

Both he and Charlie looked back and saw the cat perched up on the wall. It was sitting there as large as life, watching their every move. It had something in its mouth, something big. As Zak and Charlie approached, it glared down at them and dropped its prize at their feet.

'Ughhh! Disgusting!' Charlie groaned.

It was a rat – a large, dead rat with a long, snake-like tail.

Zak turned to Charlie. 'I wonder if the cat's got a name.'

As if in reply, a loud rapping sounded on the window. Mrs B was still there. She must have read Zak's mind. She was shouting something, but it was only just possible to hear what she was saying.

'Killroy,' she was saying. 'His name is Killroy! Keep him by you!'

7

Trouble at the Mill

Zak looked up at the sign above the shop window:

A. KHAN POST OFFICE GROCERIES

'Come on! They'll know in here,' Zak said.

He walked into the shop, closely followed by Charlie. Inside, there was a strange concoction of smells: food, newspapers, sweets and cleaning agents.

Zak looked over the sweets, but all the time glancing up at the post office counter. An Asian man stood behind the glass sorting through some papers. Otherwise, the shop was empty.

The man spotted Zak. 'Not seen you in here before. Are you visiting?'

'No, I just moved here,' Zak replied. 'A few days ago.'

'Not me though,' Charlie pointed out. 'I'm just visiting.'

Zak picked up a strawberry-flavoured toffee stick. 'I think I'll have this!'

Charlie still hadn't made his mind up. He continued to scan the sweet selection.

The shopkeeper smiled. 'I'll be with you in a minute.'

'I'll ask him,' Zak mumbled under his breath. 'Leave it to me.'

Charlie nodded.

'So . . . won't be long before you lads are back at school!' the shopkeeper said, appearing between two racks of canned food.

Zak thought for a moment. 'Oh . . . yes! We start back on Monday.' He showed the shopkeeper the toffee bar and held out fifty pence. 'Do you know where Greenlands is?'

The Asian man took Zak's money and nodded. 'The old mill. It's down by the river. A fifteen-minute walk from here. Why do you want to know?'

'Just heard someone mention it,' Zak said casually.

The man gave Zak his change, and then took Charlie's money – he'd chosen a chocolate bar. 'It closed down years ago. There's not much there now, just old boarded-up buildings, the railway and the river. Take my advice and stay away. It's a spooky old place . . . dangerous and full of ghosts.'

The mention of ghosts caused both Zak and Charlie to jerk their heads up. The shopkeeper smiled kindly at them. 'Just an expression, lads! I could just as easily have said "full of memories". Same thing!'

They thanked the shopkeeper and walked out.

'If we head back to the traffic lights and turn left, the road goes down to the level crossing and on to the river. Sounds like the mill's down that way.'

Charlie broke off a piece of chocolate and shoved it in his mouth. 'Shall we go and have a look?'

'Yep. Let's get a move on. It'll be lunchtime before we know it.'

Five minutes later, the boys had crossed the level crossing and were standing on the road bridge, looking downstream. There was nothing to see, just flat grassy fields bordering the fast-flowing river – the fields looked pale and yellow under the wintry sun.

'Cross over,' Zak instructed his friend. 'We'll have a look the other way.'

They carefully crossed the busy road and looked upstream. Charlie was the first to spot a building with a very tall chimney. 'There!' he exclaimed, pointing into the distance. 'What do you reckon?'

Zak took a bite of his toffee bar and spoke with his mouth full. 'Yep! That's it. It's got to be.'

The two friends climbed over a stile at the side of the stone bridge and descended a faint path down to the riverside. Zak looked towards the distant building – it didn't seem too far away! And then he glanced up at the sky – it was clear, but on the horizon a mass of grey cloud loomed ominously.

'Let's get a move on before it rains!'

They trudged on up the river bank, their feet crunching on the frosted remains of the rotting bank-side vegetation. As they drew closer, Zak saw that the tall chimney was square with a round bit on top. The mill building was grey and grimy with lots of big windows, each made up of small square panes, many of them broken. It reminded Zak of some grim prison building. 'That place is already giving me the creeps!' he muttered as butterflies invaded his stomach.

'I know what you mean,' Charlie replied, staring ahead.

Five minutes later the path left the river side and led up to a lane, which in turn crossed the river via a rusted iron bridge.

'Come on!' Zak said, spurring Charlie on. 'That looks like the way into the mill.'

The boys made their way up and crossed over the iron bridge, soon reaching a big gateway on their left; it led into a huge cobbled yard with the main mill building and tall chimney on the far side of it.

Zak stood to attention, hands by his sides, staring across the yard. 'That guy in the shop was right . . . definitely spooky!'

'Exactly right!' Charlie said, moving up beside him.

The gate was open. They moved cautiously through it to the middle of the yard, their trainers treading silently over the old cobbles.

The grim building looked even darker close up . . . almost black with grime. The windows that were smashed were boarded up from the inside; those that were still intact were encrusted with dirt and impossible to see through. At ground level there were lots of metal doors, some single, some double, all weather-beaten and rusted with traces of green paint flaking off.

'So now what?' Charlie asked, almost in a whisper.

'We look for The Ferret?' Zak replied. He scanned the building. Most of the doors were padlocked. But one of the doors was slightly open; it creaked and groaned as it swung in the stiffening breeze. A faded sign over the doorway read:

GREENLANDS AND CO.

'Let's take a look in there,' Zak suggested.

In the same instant, a gust of wind came out of nowhere, whistled around the yard and made a distinct whining sound. The open door slammed shut. Zak tensed. His senses seemed to be telling him that he and Charlie were not alone.

He looked up at the sky. Grey clouds had appeared, crowding in and shutting out the friendly blue colour. Spits of rain began to fall. The wind strengthened.

'Come on . . . let's see if we can open that door.'

Charlie forced a smile. 'OK . . . if you say so!'

The rain started to fall more sharply. Zak crept over to the door and tried the handle. It wouldn't open. He peered through the windows on either side. It was impossible to see anything – the glass was either frosted or too dirty to see through. They walked along the edge of the building trying other doors without success. Eventually, they reached the far side of the building where it stood alongside the railway. A familiar sound echoed in the distance.

'A train!' Charlie exclaimed.

'That'll be the Leeds train,' Zak informed him.

The boys leaned on a stout wooden fence and watched as the diesel sped towards them. It passed by at great speed. The ground rattled. Their ears rattled. The butterflies in Zak's stomach melted away. Everything seemed normal again . . . until Zak turned and looked back.

His heart turned to ice as he saw the small boy standing in the open doorway, where the door had slammed shut. He recognised the boy immediately. He was waving, beckoning Zak towards him.

Zak gripped Charlie by the shoulder, 'Look!'

Charlie swung round, but the door had slammed shut again. There was nothing to see.

Zak couldn't help himself. He sprinted towards the door.

'What's going on?' Charlie gasped, chasing after him.

'That boy . . . the one I saw at the end of my bed . . . I just saw him again! We've got to get to him.'

'Yeah, but look at that!' Charlie yelled from behind.

Zak detected the panic in Charlie's voice. He turned round and saw where he was pointing. A big metal sign high up on the wall warned:

THIS AREA IS MONITORED BY CCTV AND PATROLLED BY DOGS.

Zak swallowed hard. He felt annoyed with himself for not spotting the sign earlier. Some detective!

He scanned around the yard again. A pile of old bricks and masonry stood in one corner. In another corner, the blackened remains of a bonfire and a couple of old oil drums, which looked as if they had been used as seats. In another part of the yard, a waste skip was filled with all manner of rubbish. Some corrugated sheets were stacked against a wall. But no signs of life.

He strained his ears . . . apart from the wind moaning around the yard, everything was deathly quiet. 'If there *is* anyone around it'll be the security man,' Zak said sternly, trying to sound sure of himself.

'You mean The Ferret!'

Zak nodded, 'And *he's* the one we're looking for. So I still think we should try that door. He was there – the ghost-boy – I saw him.'

'Just . . . just hang on . . .' Charlie stammered.

Zak ignored him and walked up to the door. His heart beat faster. He pulled on it with all his strength. It opened.

Charlie screamed from behind: 'Zak!'

Zak swung around.

A huge dog – Zak recognised it as a Rottweiler – was edging around the side of the waste skip. It growled savagely, never taking its eyes off them. Before either boy could say anything, it lurched forward, barking loudly and baring its teeth.

Charlie froze. Zak grabbed him, dragged him through the open door . . . and pulled it shut. Seconds later, they grimaced as heavy paws pounded on the metal. Zak whirled round, remembering the boy he'd seen in the doorway. But there was no one . . . just a huge dark space with a cold grey concrete floor; it was littered with old newspapers and several empty milk bottles. In a far corner of the room, an open doorway stood in shadow.

Zak looked at Charlie.

Charlie frowned, staring back with big eyes – not even a hint of a smile. 'I don't like this, Zak. We've got to get out of here . . . back to yours. Mum will be coming for me soon.'

Outside, the dog stopped barking. Everything went quiet . . . only the sound of rain splattering on the grimy glass panes.

'Don't worry!' Zak said reassuringly. 'We'll find a way out.'

'Did . . . did you really see him . . . the ghost-boy?' Charlie stammered. 'You sounded really freaked out!'

'Yes,' Zak replied, 'it was definitely him! Come on . . . follow me!'

As Zak set off towards the door space in the corner, he

accidentally kicked over a milk bottle. The clattering sound set the dog off barking again.

With Charlie right behind him, they crept on to the far corner and through into the next room. It was another huge space, but this one wasn't empty. A massive piece of machinery took up most of the floor space. It consisted of several huge rollers stacked sideways on top of each other, their long curved surfaces covered in sharp metal spikes. There were metal grids and other strange-looking parts in all sorts of places – the whole thing rusted and draped in spiders' webs.

'Blimey! What's that?' Charlie asked.

Zak's imagination went into overdrive. 'It looks like some sort of torture instrument . . . like a rack . . . for stretching people.'

Charlie took off his glasses and wiped them. 'Brilliant! That's really cheered me up!'

'Sorry!' Zak apologised. 'We'd better keep moving. Look . . . that red door over there . . . it's open.'

They crept on past the monstrous machine, Zak constantly looking ahead, wondering if the ghost-boy was going to pop up again.

Charlie stopped and grabbed Zak's arm. 'Listen!'

But Zak had already heard it. From close behind, the sound of the outside metal door rattled open . . . followed by the savage barking and whining of the Rottweiler.

'Oh no!' Zak cried out. 'It's in!'

'We're dead!' Charlie screamed.

'RUN!' Zak screamed louder.

He pulled Charlie towards the red door, praying that it wouldn't be locked . . . that they could get through and slam it shut. But to his horror, it opened before they got there.

The pale figure of the boy barred the doorway . . . tapping the side of his ghostly head with a ghostly hand . . . trying to shout something . . . but making no sound.

Zak stopped dead in his tracks. Charlie crashed into him and the two of them went sprawling onto the concrete floor. The deafening barking of the Rottweiler rang in their ears. They rolled over and shrieked in terror as the beast's slavering jaws loomed over them.

8

The Ferret

Zak closed his eyes and clenched his teeth, ready to be mauled . . . then nothing happened!

'Steady, Rufus! What 'ave you found 'ere, boy?'

Zak opened his eyes and much to his relief saw that the dog's head had been jerked back. The Rottweiler was attached to a thick, leather leash and a small ageing man wearing a grubby yellow safety jacket and an even grubbier baseball cap was holding him hard.

'And who might you be?' the man asked, his eyes deep-set and shifting around nervously.

Zak jerked his head round – the ghost-boy had gone . . . vanished! Then he looked back to the man. The dog was still pulling and yelping, desperate to get at them, but he held the dog easily. The handler looked old, but he was obviously strong.

'I'm Zak Freeman and this is my friend . . .'

'Charlie Mann!' Charlie chipped in.

The two friends staggered to their feet and dusted themselves down. The dog stopped pulling, sat on its haunches and panted heavily.

'Good lad, Rufus!' the man said, patting the dog's head. 'Nowt much to fear 'ere, boy – just two young 'uns having a snoop round. Asking for trouble!'

'We're looking for The Ferret,' Zak said as bravely as he could.

The man stared back at him and Zak took in his striking features – thin pointed face, rows of frown lines creasing his forehead, eyes piercing and strong. 'Well you've found 'im!'

'Mrs B said we'd find you here,' Charlie said in a friendly way.

'So you've been talking to 'er, 'ave yer? Nutty as a fruitcake!'

Charlie laughed out loud – though Zak detected it was more of a nervous laugh. 'Do they really call you The Ferret?' he asked, his face beaming.

The man scanned around the room. 'They do, lad . . . and you'd do well to stop asking questions and get yerself out of 'ere. This is no place for young lads . . . or anyone else for that matter!'

'But we need to talk to you,' Zak went on. 'Mrs B said you'd be able to help us. We want to find out about Jack.'

The Ferret looked at Zak suspiciously. 'So she sent yer to see me, did she? Well you'd better follow me then.' He yanked at the dog's lead, pulled it to its feet and walked on past the two boys through the red door where Zak had seen the ghost-boy. The two friends followed close on his heels; neither of them spoke.

Once through the door, they entered another vast empty chamber with a cold concrete floor; the room was dimly lit, just a little natural light from outside filtering through the numerous cracked and grimy windows.

'This was the main factory floor,' The Ferret said over his shoulder. 'A good few folk 'ave worked their socks off in 'ere over the years.'

'What did they do?' Zak asked as they walked on.

'Textiles,' The Ferret answered. 'This room was where Old Jenny worked.'

'Who was Old Jenny?' Charlie asked.

'She was a mean machine,' the man croaked without looking back. 'The workers depended on 'er . . . cared for 'er every whim, they did!'

Charlie cast a bemused glance at Zak. Zak shrugged his shoulders.

'We saw a big machine back in that other room,' Zak said, pointing behind them. 'What was that for?'

The man looked back to where Zak was pointing. 'That big rusty 'eap of metal was the carding machine. A friend of mine lost his hand in that. Still . . . could 'ave been worse . . . could 'ave lost 'is arm!'

Wow! It really is some sort of torture instrument! Zak thought to himself.

He was just about to ask for some more info on the sinister-looking machine when the Rottweiler let out a loud bark. Zak almost had a heart attack. The handler stopped dead in his tracks and patted the dog's head. 'Steady, Rufus . . . steady, boy!'

Zak and Charlie watched in awe as the Rottweiler stood rooted to the spot. It growled ferociously and sat to attention.

The man glanced over his shoulder at the two boys. 'Keep dead still.'

Zak stood stiffly in his 'soldier boy' stance. He looked down at the dog and his heart began to beat faster; the fur on the back of its neck was standing on end. Maybe Rufus had sensed the presence of the figure he'd seen earlier.

'What's wrong?' Charlie whispered.

The man crouched low and pointed to a shadowy corner of the room. 'There's a rat over yonder,' he whispered back. 'It's attacking a piece of cheese I put there yesterday.' The dog growled again. 'Quiet, boy!'

Before either of the boys could say or do anything else, the man eased off his yellow jacket and placed it on the floor by his side. He rolled up his sleeves to reveal thin wiry arms covered in tattoos. One of the tattoos said in big letters 'THE FERRET'.

'What are you going to do?' Zak whispered.

The man put a finger to his lips and beckoned Zak and Charlie to keep low. He pushed his hand down on the dog's head. The Rottweiler seemed to know what was about to happen and lay silently with his head resting on his outstretched paws. Without another word The Ferret sprinted forward. For someone so old, he moved with incredible stealth and speed. A scuffle ensued in the far dark corner and seconds

later, the wiry man returned holding a large rat by its tail. The
rodent dangled from his hand and struggled and squirmed.
Rufus went mad, barking frantically and rearing up on his
haunches.

'So now yer know why folk around these parts call me
"The Ferret". And I'm still as fast as I ever was. But the real
secret is to move quiet-like. They never 'ear me comin'. Years
ago, when I worked in this mill, they gave me a penny for
every one of these beggars I caught. One week it was twelve –
earned me a shilling that did!'

Zak squirmed as The Ferret dropped the wriggling rat
at Rufus's feet. The dog scooped it up in its large mouth,
crunched it and killed it in an instant.

The Ferret slipped back into his yellow jacket. 'Come on
. . . follow me!' he instructed the two startled friends.

He led them through yet another door in the corner. 'In
'ere, you two . . .' he called after them. 'Come in and sit
yerselves down.'

This time it was only a small room . . . and quite dark.
There was an old wooden desk with a blue plastic chair
behind it, two crates in front of it and an old filing cabinet
tucked away in a corner. Some half-used candles stood in a
jam jar, along with some other odds and ends, on a grubby
window ledge beneath a single grubby window.

The Ferret sat at the desk and gestured to the boys to sit on
the crates. Rufus skulked into a corner and lapped water from
a plastic bowl.

'So what do yer know about Jack?' the old man asked,
folding his arms and leaning back in his chair.

Zak looked up at the window above The Ferret's head.

Most of the little panes were draped in fine spiders' webs. 'I don't really know anything,' Zak replied. 'That's why we're here. We want to find out.'

The man leaned forward, took off his baseball cap and stared hard into Zak's eyes. 'Why do yer want to know? You 'aven't seen 'im, 'ave you?'

'Yes . . . I think I've seen him twice.'

'Well I never!'

'He saw him at the end of his bed,' Charlie piped up cheerfully.

The Ferret scratched his head and looked serious. 'That must 'ave put the wind up yer!'

'It did!' Zak confirmed. 'And I saw him again . . . here . . . just before you turned up, standing in that doorway back there.' He pointed back to the red door.

The Ferret frowned and looked even more serious. 'I've never seen 'im. But Rufus always tells me when 'e's around. I don't know whether he sees 'im or just senses 'im. Animals 'ave the knack, see . . . they can tune in to spirits and ghosts and suchlike. It's their ears . . . they can 'ear a pin drop at forty yards.'

Zak looked at his watch. Time was getting on. 'So can you tell us about Jack?'

The Ferret got up and went over to the filing cabinet. There was a small camping stove placed on top of it. He began fiddling with it. He took a box of matches from his trouser pocket. 'Jack used to work 'ere,' he said, lighting the stove.

Zak fidgeted impatiently as the man poured water from a plastic bottle into a small grubby-looking kettle.

'The lad was only twelve years old. They started 'em young

in those days. The Craddocks were a big family, see! They all had to work to keep themselves fed and clothed.'

'So what happened to him?' Zak asked, glancing at Charlie.

'And why is he a ghost?' Charlie added.

The Ferret placed the kettle on the stove, went into a deep drawer in the desk and took out three mugs. 'I'll tell yer over a cup o' tea. How do yer like it . . . milk . . . sugar?'

A few minutes later, the three of them sat sipping hot tea. The big dog stretched out beside the desk, his huge head resting on his paws. The Ferret reached into the desk again and took out a tin. He opened it and offered it to the two boys. It was full of chocolate biscuits. Zak took one and bit into the smooth dark chocolate; Charlie did the same.

Outside, black rain clouds closed in and the room grew darker. The Ferret lit one of the candles and placed it on a saucer on the window ledge. Three ghostly shadows danced on the wall in the flickering candlelight as The Ferret began his story.

'The story goes that Jack was a good lad. He worked hard. He was a scavenger . . . like most of the kids.'

'What's a scavenger?' Charlie interrupted.

The man slicked back his thinning grey hair; his eyes flitted nervously around the room. He ignored the question and continued. 'That boy would have done anything for 'is family. They lived up in the village . . . in Steetley.'

'In School Street?' Zak asked.

The Ferret nodded his pointed rodent-like head. 'Yes . . . top end.'

Zak turned to Charlie. 'That's our end.'

Charlie munched on his biscuit and nodded, his freckles standing out in the candlelight.

'Anyway . . . things were bad enough to start with. But things got really bad when the strike came.'

'What strike?' Zak asked.

'The Greenland family – they owned the mill – they 'ad money problems. 'T any rate, they decided to give the workers a pay cut . . . no warning . . . just like that!'

'So the workers went on strike,' Charlie said, reaching out for another biscuit.

Rufus was on his feet again, ears erect . . . but this time only to the sound of the biscuit tin being passed round. The Ferret took out a biscuit and offered it to the Rottweiler.

'They went on strike for ten weeks . . . almost starving, some of 'em.'

'And Jack's family?' Zak asked nervously.

A great frown spread across The Ferret's face. 'They 'ad it worst of all. Jack's little sister, see, Mary, she took ill. Consumption it was.'

'What's "Consumption"?' Zak asked.

'Lung disease . . . poor mite! She needed medicine and that cost money.'

'Couldn't they get it from the chemist on a prescription?' Charlie asked, his voice full of concern.

The Ferret sipped his tea, his eyes staring over the rim of his mug. 'Not in those days, son. Those with money survived . . . and those without struggled. In any case, she needed more than medicine. She needed clean air, and that cost the family even more money.'

The boys looked puzzled.

The Ferret continued. 'They 'ad to get Mary away, see . . . to the seaside. That's what people did in those days if they could afford it. Along with the medicine, the clean sea air 'elped get rid of the disease.'

'So Mary didn't . . . die . . . did she?' Zak stammered.

'No. Jack saw to that.'

'How?' Charlie asked.

'He worked?'

'But . . . you said they were on strike . . .'

''Is family sneaked 'im through the picket line.'

'What's a picket line?' Zak asked.

'It's when the workers stand outside the factory waving banners and stuff and they won't let anyone go in to work,' Charlie stated proudly. 'We did our own history projects at school. You did yours on steam trains, Zak . . . do you remember? I did mine on the miners' strike.'

Zak nodded.

'Impressive, son!' The Ferret said with the faintest of smiles on his stern features. 'And maybe yer know that folk on a picket line don't take kindly to anyone trying to get through?'

Charlie nodded. 'Some miners got beaten up for that. And after the strike people wouldn't even speak to them.'

'Well you can see why they'd be upset!' Zak said.

The Ferret's eyes darted around nervously again. 'You're right . . . it stinks! "Scabs"! That's what they call folk who break the picket line. Why should they carry on working and earning while other folk are starving for what they believe is just and right? It beggars belief!' He took a long slurp from his mug of tea. 'But when yer kid sister is dying . . . well . . . maybe that's different!'

'Did they call him Scabbajack?' Zak asked, thinking back to the girls' skipping game in his dream.

'Oh I see . . . because he became a "Scab"!' Charlie added.

The Ferret nodded. 'That's right! The strike lasted for ten weeks and Jack worked for seven of 'em. But it cost 'im dearly!'

The candle on the window ledge started flickering. The dog moved into a sitting position. Zak sensed the sudden change in the atmosphere . . . more eerie . . . more tense.

The Ferret's eyes scanned around the room. 'One of the mill workers was a nasty piece of work. 'Is name was Murdoch . . . Bill Murdoch. 'E was a Supervisor, or "Overlooker" as they called 'em in those days. He was also the Union Man.'

'What's a Union Man?' Charlie asked.

The Ferret frowned. 'The Union Man is the one who's supposed to look after the interests of the workers. But Murdoch was only ever interested in 'imself. 'E was a drunkard and a bully . . . a troublemaker with a vicious temper. 'E was the one who put the workers on strike – it was right up 'is street – he revelled in it. And as soon as 'e 'eard about young Jack being a scab, it made 'is blood boil. 'E tried to get folk to gang up on 'im . . . on 'is family. Told 'em if Jack went into work again 'e'd regret it . . . they'd regret it . . . the family, like.'

The candle flickered again. The room was growing darker. Their shadows danced wildly on the walls. Zak sensed that The Ferret's story was drawing to a dreadful climax. By the look on Charlie's face, he sensed the same.

'And so what happened?' Zak demanded impatiently.

'Most of the strikers turned a blind eye. They felt sorry for the Craddocks. The family were well-liked, see. So young Jack kept sneaking in. His sister was sent away to the coast and straight away she began to get better. But the family needed money . . . to keep 'er there.'

'But when he sneaked into work, how could he do all the jobs himself?' Zak asked.

'The Greenland family rallied together. And what with a few other strike breakers and young Jack chipping in, they managed to turn out a few o' the goods. In any case, the mill owner was legally obliged to pay folk who turned up for work.'

It was Charlie's turn to sound agitated now. 'So . . . so what happened?'

The Ferret banged his mug down on the desk. 'Jack disappeared . . . off the face of the earth. Story goes that his Uncle Albert sneaked him in to work early one morning, and the boy never came home. He was never seen again!'

'What do you think happened to him,' Zak asked almost reluctantly. He wasn't sure he wanted to know.

The old man looked anxious. The candle struggled to keep alight. Rufus was on his feet now, his ears erect. 'Oh, I know what 'appened. All the folk around these parts knows what 'appened. And they knew then! It's just that folk didn't dare speak out lest the same thing should 'appen to them. Murdoch was evil and vicious. 'E was twice the size of a normal man and as strong as an ox. Folk were in fear of 'im. So the murdering scumbag got away with it.'

Zak suddenly saw the image of the ghost-boy in his mind . . . that frightened look . . . the eyes full of fear . . . of dread.

'So what 'appened . . . I mean "happened"?' Charlie asked, breaking the spell.

'Murdoch . . . he did away with 'im . . . murdered the poor young wretch. They say 'e killed him with a cleaver. Chopped 'is body up. Murdoch was a lodger with a butcher, see.'

'A butcher?' Zak gasped.

The Ferret nodded and took another sip of his tea. 'Old Jud . . .'e was old and kept pretty much to 'imself. They reckon that Jud didn't 'ave a clue what the big man was up to.'

Zak's mind reeled with images of the stone table in the cellar . . . the hooks in the ceiling . . . the big man chopping the meat. 'I saw him. It was him . . . Murdoch . . . in our cellar . . . he was chopping something up!'

Charlie gasped. 'I can't believe it! So Murdoch really killed Jack?'

The Ferret nodded and glanced nervously from Zak to Charlie. 'Like I said . . . Bill Murdoch was evil.'

The candle flickered wildly and went out. The natural light from the window had all but gone. Rufus stood silent, tense, his ears erect.

'There's ghosts around,' The Ferret whispered, 'Rufus can 'ear 'em.'

'I wouldn't have your job for all the money in the world,' Charlie said quietly. 'Don't you get scared?'

The Ferret shook his head. 'I get nervous . . . who wouldn't? But with Rufus around I think I'm safe enough.' He cast a glance at Zak. 'Strikes me that you're the one that should be on your guard, son.'

Zak tensed. 'What do you mean?'

The Ferret got up and relit the candle. ''Cos you're the one that sees things. I bet yer pal doesn't, do yer, lad?' He looked at Charlie.

'I haven't seen anything yet.' Charlie replied, shaking his head.

'No . . . and you won't do. Those that see are the ones who are meant to. Yer pal's meant to . . . maybe for a reason.'

'But Mrs B said that Jack would never hurt anyone,' Zak spoke up with a slight tremble in his voice.

The two friends watched in silence as The Ferret fastened the lead back onto the dog's collar and set off towards the door. 'She's right. It would be the ghost of Bill Murdoch I'd be afeared of. Spawned by Satan that one! They say that after 'e chopped Jack's body up, 'e sneaked out one night and dumped it in the river. Ask Mrs B . . . she'll tell yer that on certain nights the old millstream runs red with the lad's blood.'

Zak's heart began to race. An awful thought had entered his mind. 'Just tell me one more thing,' he said. 'Where did Murdoch and the butcher live and how come you know Mrs B?'

'That's *two* things!' The Ferret said, standing in the doorway. 'I know a lot about Mrs B . . . or The Widow Blackham . . . whatever you want to call her. I should do . . . she's my mother. And if Jack Craddock had lived, he would have been my uncle.'

Zak's head whirled. He struggled to get his head around it.

'And when my mother was a young lass, the murdering scumbag and the butcher lived right next door to her.'

Zak's head reeled. The Ferret's words struck ice into his heart. No wonder he'd seen the vision of Murdoch standing by the stone table. Murdoch had lived in Zak's house, 21 School Street!

9

Ultimate Nightmare

Back at Zak's, Charlie's mum was waiting. The boys had agreed to say nothing of their adventures, but Mrs Mann noticed immediately that her son looked agitated. Charlie put it down to having to rush to get back on time and his mum accepted it.

As soon as they left, Zak made his way down to his writing den.

The afternoon was dark – it was more like night – and when Zak saw Killroy sitting on the wall by the shed, he remembered Mrs B's words:

Keep the cat close!

It wasn't difficult to tempt Killroy inside. The shed had a heater and the cat seemed to know it. As soon as Zak switched it on, Killroy curled up by the side of it and purred contentedly. Five minutes later, Zak was fully concentrating on the next instalment of his writing:

Ghost Sightings

I've seen the boy.

I'm not making this up. He was really there . . . at the end of my bed. His face haunts my every waking moment, a mixture of sadness and terror. When I looked into his eyes I wanted to scream and cry at the same time.

I think he needs my help.

I don't know why . . . or how . . . but I'm sure of it. I feel his presence more and more. Wherever I go, he is close. I saw him again today, at the old mill, standing in a doorway, that same look of despair and hope on his pale white face.

How can I help him? He tries to speak, but makes no sound.

Charlie was scared . . . who wouldn't be? But Charlie doesn't see him. The Ferret, Rufus, and the old cat, Killroy . . . they all sense him . . . but they don't see him either.

Only I see him. Why?

Was he really murdered, just because he wanted to work hard to save his sister's life? That would be so cruel.

And worst of all . . . did the murderer really live in our house? I swear I'll never go down the cellar again . . . ever!

At that moment, Killroy stirred . . . sat up and glanced around. The temperature in the shed suddenly dropped and a chill spread through the air. Zak put his hand on the heater – it was still warm – but the shed felt cold.

'What's wrong?' Zak asked, staring at the cat's twitching whiskery face.

Outside, it was still dark and blustery. Killroy was on his feet now, looking towards the door, his back beginning to arch.

Zak took the hint. He hurriedly shut down his PC and packed his stuff away. He decided he'd had enough scares for one day.

'Come on, boy!'

He opened the door and the cat shot out. Zak followed quickly after him.

'Good timing, Zak! I've made you a cup of tea and toasted a teacake.'

The sound of Mum's voice calling from up the garden cheered him up no end . . . and he loved toasted teacakes. He sped on up the garden, and never looked back . . . though he had the strongest feeling that someone was behind him . . . watching his every move!

*

That night Zak was very tired. He knew he needed a good night's sleep. But from the moment he drifted into slumber, the nightmare started.

He found himself back at Greenlands Mill, but this time on his own. He entered the barren factory site and began searching for the ghost-boy, but there was no sign of anyone.

He slipped through a metal door and scoured the network of empty spaces. The wind moaned outside, whistling into the cold rooms through smashed windowpanes, chilling the air and causing Zak to shiver as he continued his fruitless search.

He crept into the room with the huge 'torture machine'. He edged past it, looked up at one of the grimy windows and saw a dark shadowy face staring in at him. His heart raced as he ran outside to confront the watcher . . . but there was no one there. The cobbled yard was deserted. And then he saw the ghost-boy peering from behind an old rubbish skip in the corner. But when he ran over, the boy had disappeared again. Again and again the boy appeared and disappeared and Zak chased after him, becoming more and more frustrated, crying out in his nightmare:

'WHY ARE YOU FOLLOWING ME? WHAT DO YOU WANT? TELL ME!'

Finally, he gave up. He walked out of the yard and over to the iron footbridge crossing the river. He stopped on the bridge to look down at the water and felt a tap on his shoulder. He jumped around. The ghost-boy was standing there . . . his deathly-white face only inches from his own. The boy screamed a shrill scream so loud that Zak's ears felt about to burst. And then Zak tried to scream . . . but no sound would come out . . . just overwhelming silence.

In bed, Zak broke out in a cold sweat and tossed and turned.

The boy with the pale white face and cherry-red lips tapped the side of his head with two fingers, his other hand pointing down over the side of the bridge. Zak swung round, looked down and saw a sinister figure crouched by the water. It was a man – a big man with a large round head and broad back. He had a sack by his side and it was obvious that he was up to no good. As Zak continued to stare, the man turned and gazed up at him. Even from up on the bridge, Zak saw his awful features clearly – deep-set eyes, twisted nose and snarling mouth, set in an expression of pure malice. There was no doubt in Zak's mind that this was the face of Bill Murdoch – Jack's murderer.

Zak turned back. The ghost-boy was still standing there, silent and rigid, staring with eyes like saucers. He took hold of Zak's arm and pushed something cold into the palm of his hand. Zak looked down and saw a silver disc . . . some sort of coin or medal.

This was all too much. Zak decided to make a run for it . . . away from the two spectres of his nightmare . . . *but where to go?*

He dashed across the bridge, scrambled down the far river bank and sprinted alongside the fast-moving water, constantly glancing behind. The ghost-boy faded away and disappeared . . . but then, to his horror, he saw that the big man was already halfway across the bridge and starting after him. Worse still, he was waving something in a threatening way. Zak knew exactly what it was – *a cleaver* – its sharp blade covered in blood.

Zak gasped, his heart beating to bursting point. He tried to sprint faster, but the ground had become marshy and his legs wouldn't respond; instead, his limbs grew heavier with every step. A side stream appeared and he ran beside it, the water burbling and gurgling, echoing his own sounds of distress. The ground grew soggier. His feet began to sink and his legs almost gave up, but the grunts and curses of his pursuer rang into the cold night air and spurred him on. Suddenly, the stream changed direction and swung round in front of him. He had to leap across it. There was no other way.

In desperation, he hurled himself into the air. But his energy had sapped and he dropped like a stone into the freezing cold water. His limp body swirled beneath the torrent, his lungs fit to burst as he held his breath for what seemed an eternity. And then he bobbed like a cork to the surface . . . *a blood-red watery surface!*

Worse still, Jack's detached head floated beside him – its lifeless eyes staring into nothingness, a fixed expression of terror on its dead face. Zak gasped and spluttered as it drifted around him in the swirling current, turning and gyrating like some grotesque fairground ride.

And then Zak woke up.

He sat bolt upright in bed, mixed feelings of horror and relief sweeping through him. He was sweating but shivering. This nightmare had been terrifying. But thank goodness it had only been a nightmare . . . *and yet it had all seemed so real.*

He took some deep breaths, sighed, looked around, and lay down again. It was only then that he realised his left hand was clenched in a fist. He was holding onto something.

He sat up again and slowly opened his fingers. A silver disc glistened in the palm of his hand.

10

Back to School

Zak liked his new school.

Everyone at Airedale High seemed friendly – both teachers and pupils had made the 'new boy' very welcome. And being back at school had given Zak some sort of normality to his life. The bizarre happenings of the last few days already seemed distant and dreamlike.

Zak was sitting in the school library.

A cold winter sun shone in through the big airy windows lighting up the rows and rows of bookshelves. A joy to Zak's eyes! The far side of the library was an area for study – smart oak tables topped with PCs and lots of pupils working away. Zak was sitting in a more restful area at the front of the library – low comfy chairs and low tables – perfect for reading in peace. He was looking through a book entitled *Textile Mills of the Aire Valley*.

'You must be the new boy.'

Zak looked up.

My name's Mrs Hardwick. I'm the librarian. What's your name?'

'Zak Freeman, Miss.' He took in the lady's smart appearance – smooth black skirt, a cream patterned blouse and gold-rimmed spectacles adorning her kind smiling face. Her hair was cut short and neat and had a gold tinge to it, which matched her specs. She glanced down at the book he was holding.

'Well, Zak! It's good to see you in here on your first day. You're obviously into books. But why Textile Mills?'

'There's an old mill near to our house. I just wanted to find out about it.'

Mrs Hardwick folded her arms across her neat blouse and smiled. 'Where do you live?'

Zak sensed that the librarian was genuinely interested in pupils – not just books! 'Steetley, Miss.'

'Ah . . . well! You're referring to Greenlands, then. It was a thriving place in the community years ago . . . not the spooky old place it is now. You might find a few references to it, but I can probably tell you as much as you need to know. I'm a bit of an expert on local history. Most of my family worked at the mill in the old days. Do you mind if I sit down for a minute?'

Zak sat up straight. 'No . . . fine.' He took to the librarian instantly. 'I had a look around Greenlands a few days ago. I went to meet someone,' he added quickly. 'I went there with my friend and we met The Ferret . . . er . . . I mean . . . the security man. He showed us around.'

Mrs Hardwick pursed her lips. She looked more than interested. 'Probably not much to see now, is there? The machines were all taken away and sold . . . or scrapped.'

'Except for one,' Zak said. He described the big machine he'd seen in one of the rooms. He said how it reminded him of some sort of torture instrument.

'Ah, that would have been the carding machine,' she laughed.

'Yes, that's what *he* said . . . The Ferret.'

'Why on earth do they call him The Ferret?' she asked, screwing up her face.

Zak told her how the security man had caught a rat with his bare hands and she screwed up her face even more. Now it was Zak's turn to laugh. 'What is a carding machine, anyway?' He chuckled.

'Well, when the wool arrived at the mill, some of the women and children would pick through it first and get all the rough stuff out by hand – they were called "pickers". And then the carding machine, with its big spiky cylinders, was used to comb the wool and straighten out all the fibres ready for spinning.'

Zak nodded thoughtfully. 'Did many children work in the mill?'

The librarian sighed. 'At one time, there were more children working in mills than adults. Children as young as six used to work there. Eventually, the government insisted on children going to school until they were fourteen, but even then their parents still sent them to the mills to work part-time. They were known as "half-timers" and children as young as eleven did a shift in the mill and half a day at school right until the 1920s.

'Incredible!' Jack said. 'What kind of jobs did they do?'

Mrs Hardwick's face took on a sad expression. 'The worst ones! Apart from helping with the picking, some of them had the job of ducking under the moving machinery to collect bits of wool and fibre . . . nothing was wasted.'

'That sounds dangerous.'

'It was!' The librarian sighed. 'They were known as "Scavengers". Some of the poor mites had terrible accidents – hair, arms and legs getting trapped in the moving parts of the machinery – doesn't bear thinking about.'

'Nasty!' Zak agreed.

'The working conditions were horrendous . . . the air full of dust and fibres . . . everyone breathing it in! Their lungs must have been full of it.'

'That's really bad.'

The librarian was now staring into space. She'd transported herself back in time, to the mill. 'My Uncle Jim . . . he's dead now . . . he was stone deaf. He worked in the mill all his life. It was the loom . . . the Spinning Jenny . . . it was deafening. The workers rarely spoke to each other.'

Something clicked in Zak's mind. *Old Jenny*. Hadn't The Ferret mentioned her?

An electronic sound brought the librarian out of her trance. 'Ah well, Zak! That's morning break over. It's time we were both on our way.'

Zak got up, something still troubling him. And then his brain registered . . .

'If they never spoke . . . how did they . . .?'

The librarian anticipated Zak's question. 'They read each other's lips and made signs.'

Zak tapped two fingers on the side of his head. 'Did this mean anything, Miss?'

The librarian looked amazed. 'You're quite a researcher, Zak. Where did you dig that up from?'

'Well . . . er . . .'

The librarian looked towards the door. A middle-aged man in a suit and tie stood just outside the entrance. He glanced at his watch and scanned around the library.

Mrs Hardwick looked at Zak and tapped two fingers on the side of her head. 'They used it as a signal to warn that the boss was on his way. As soon as anyone made that sign, everybody jumped and got on with their work. Bye for now!'

Zak's eyes opened wide. He picked up his belongings and made a quick exit, his mind reeling with all the information the knowledgeable Mrs Hardwick had given him. She was ten times more informative than any book in the non-fiction department. *What a find!*

When the bell sounded for the end of school, Zak ran most of the way home. He made his way straight down to his writing den (with Killroy in tow), and within minutes was tapping away on the keys of his PC.

New School, New Plans
I felt really nervous this morning, starting my new school, but it's been a great first day. The pupils and the teachers are very friendly – especially Mrs Hardwick, the librarian – I think she and I are already good friends.

She seems to know everything.

The ghost-boy (I'm going to call him Jack from now on) came to me again last night – in a dream – or should I say 'nightmare'! I'm sure he needs my help and I intend to find out why. Maybe I need to learn to lip-read!

I woke up with a silver coin in my hand. Jack put it there! It all sounds too incredible. No one would believe me . . . not even Charlie. I have to keep looking at it – even I can't believe it! It's engraved with a picture of a man. He's got a long stick and he's carrying a child on his back. I might ask Mum about it.

I've decided on a plan to get to the bottom of why Jack keeps stalking me. It's going to take a lot of courage, but I'm determined to do it. Otherwise, all this spooky stuff is going to go on for ever and drive me mad! Charlie and his mum are visiting again tomorrow. Brilliant! I'm going to discuss my plans with Charlie. Until then, I'm just going to stay on my guard and keep Killroy close. I'm not quite so scared of Jack any more – it's Murdoch that I'm terrified of. I still can't get my head round the fact that he lived in my house. One thing's for sure . . . as I said before . . . I'll never go down the cellar again!

ZF

Zak switched off the PC, ushered Killroy outside and locked up his writing den. He suddenly felt drawn to look around the back of the shed. He took a deep breath and had a quick peep. No one there! He peered over the stone wall at the back of the shed. No one there! *Phew!*

He headed towards the house. He glanced up at Mrs B's upstairs window: *she was there!*

Zak felt his heart skip a beat as the wizened old face stared down at him. He looked away quickly, but she was already tapping on the window. He really wanted to walk on, get inside the house, but that would have been rude. So he stopped, stood stiffly and turned his attention back to the window. Mrs B was waving down at him, signalling to him to stay where he was. Zak nodded and she disappeared. He waited patiently. Finally, he heard her back door open and a moment later the old face was back, peering over the garden fence.

'Did you see him . . . The Ferret?' Mrs B croaked.

Zak nodded.

'Did he tell you what you wanted to know?'

Zak nodded again. 'He also told me that you're his mother.'

The wrinkly face looked sheepish. ''S right! He's my only child. Though not such a child now, eh?' The old woman cackled like a witch again. 'And did my lad tell you how Jack met a grim end?'

Zak shivered at the thought. 'Yes! He told me that Jack was his uncle. He also told me about Jack being a scab – how he'd worked during the strike to save Mary, his young sister.'

The old face ducked down below the fence. Zak stood there, in his usual soldier-like fashion, wondering what had alarmed her. And then the face was back again, peering over the fence with tear-filled eyes.

'What's wrong?' Zak asked the old lady anxiously.

The sad mournful eyes gazed back at him. 'You seem a

smart lad. Work it out! Jack was my lad's uncle . . . what does that make Jack to me?'

Zak bit the end of his thumb and tried to work it out. Relations and all that stuff always confused him. If Jack was The Ferret's uncle and The Ferret was Mrs B's son . . . then . . . 'You and Jack were brother and sister!' Zak blurted out excitedly.

The old woman nodded gravely and disappeared, this time her door slamming shut.

Zak stood there smiling. He was so pleased with himself that he'd worked things out. He was becoming quite the detective.

He set off towards the house again . . . and stopped dead in his tracks. The smile seeped away from his face as something else dawned on him.

No wonder the old woman looked so sad . . . perhaps even guilty.

Mrs B – The Widow Blackham – was not only Jack's sister, *she was Mary!* And Jack had saved her life, but in doing so had given up his own.

11

Messages

For once, Zak slept well. No nightmares, no dreams at all . . . just a well-needed refreshing night's sleep! When he woke up, he looked at his bedside clock. Ten past eight.

'Are you awake, Zak?' Mum's voice sounded from down below.

'Yep!' He looked over to the window. The light through the curtains seemed somehow brighter. He pushed back the duvet and swung his legs out of bed. He shivered – the room seemed colder than usual. He slipped his feet into his slippers and walked over to the window.

He drew back the curtains and saw the network of thin white lines etched onto the glass. Someone's scratchy fingers had been at work! It was Jack! But this time . . . Jack Frost!

And beyond the glass, the white school playground and glistening roof tiles were further testimony to Jack's nocturnal visit. In fact, it seemed *Jack* had been everywhere!

Zak smiled to himself. Ever since a small child, the infamous Jack Frost had never failed to inspire his imagination in all sorts of ways. He rubbed his fingers on the cold pane – even on the inside it felt freezing. He noticed that some of his fingers had red stains on them. He rubbed his hands together – whatever it was wouldn't come off. He went into the bathroom and washed his hands – the red stuff still wouldn't budge. He shrugged his shoulders, finished washing and cleaned his teeth.

Downstairs, during breakfast, he checked with Mum that Charlie was still coming round.

'Yes. It's a bit of a trek for them, but Kath insisted on giving me a hand to unpack the last of the boxes. They'll be here around five and staying until about eight.'

'Great!' Zak said, thinking ahead to his plan.

'Mum . . . do you know what this is?' He slid the silver disc across the table.

Mrs Freeman picked it up and examined it. 'Yes. It's a St Christopher. It's like a lucky charm. It's supposed to keep you safe when you're travelling. See that man, he's St Christopher and he's carrying Jesus on his back.' She passed it back across the table. 'Where did you get it?'

'I found it,' Zak lied. No one would ever believe where it really came from.

He was about to change the subject when his dad walked in, went over to the kettle and clicked the switch. 'Morning, Zak! Have you been down the cellar?'

Zak screwed his face up. 'No way!'

'I doubt he would go down there again,' Mrs Freeman said. 'Not after that last episode.'

Zak stared at his father. 'Why, Dad . . . what's up?'

The switch on the kettle clicked off. Mr Freeman poured boiling water into his mug. 'You don't sleepwalk do you?'

'Why?'

'What's all this about?' Mrs Freeman asked, a degree of concern in her voice.

'You'd better take a look down there – both of you!'

Zak got up from the table and followed his mum towards the cellar door. She flicked on the light switch and crept cautiously down the steps. Zak followed close behind, his father taking up the rear. At the bottom of the steps, Mrs Freeman stopped abruptly and Zak bumped into the back of her.

'What on earth . . .!'

Zak stood by her side and gawped.

Dad's red stone paint had been got at and someone had daubed a picture on the wall by the stone table. A big stickman wielding what looked like a meat cleaver towered over a much smaller stickman lying on the floor . . . only the small stickman was in pieces . . . chopped up. Zak guessed at once that the small stickman was meant to be a boy. Jack Craddock!

'Who's done this?' Mrs Freeman asked in disbelief.

'And there's more,' her husband added. 'I came down earlier to turn the boiler up . . . that's when I found it.' He brushed past them, led them over to the fuel store and flicked on the light.

Zak's eyes widened as he saw the blood-red words daubed in big letters on the left-hand wall:

Scabbajack, Scabbajack
Zak and Jack are going back

Zak and his parents stood in silence, each trying to work out who was responsible.

'Zak!' Mrs Freeman suddenly exclaimed. She pointed down at his feet.

Zak looked down and saw that one of his slippers was covered in dried red paint. And then he opened the palm of his right hand, remembering his stained red fingers.

'What's going on, Zak?' Mr Freeman sighed.

'I . . . I . . . I don't . . . know!' Zak stammered.

Mrs Freeman looked at Zak with an expression of sympathetic concern. 'You've been acting strangely ever since we moved here. I think we need to have a little chat, don't you?' She put her arm around Zak's shoulder and led him away.

'I've got to get off to work, I'll clean this up later.' Mr Freeman called after them. 'I'll leave you some white spirit to clean Zak's hands.'

*

The school day had gone well enough, though more than once Zak had been guilty of daydreaming, preoccupied with the mysterious message in the cellar. And now Zak was home again, it was such a relief to have Charlie around to talk things over with.

Outside, the temperature had dropped to well below zero, but the inside of the shed was snug and warm. Killroy was in his usual place, curled up in front of the wall heater, purring with his eyes closed.

Charlie sat with his head back in the armchair, his face in a half-smile. 'So what did your mum and dad make of that?'

'Same as me.' Zak grunted, swivelling his desk chair backwards and forwards. 'They couldn't get their heads around it. Mum wants me to go to the doctor's. She's really worried about me.'

'Can't blame them.' Charlie beamed. 'You did a crazy thing creeping down the cellar like that. And those words daubed on the wall . . . what was all that about?'

Zak glanced at Killroy – still curled up asleep. 'I still can't believe I did it. Why would I? The only thing I can think is that it's a message . . . to me . . . from Jack,' he said sternly. 'But I don't know what it means.'

Charlie stopped smiling. His expression changed to a rare worried frown. 'So what next?'

'I'm going to try and find out exactly what this is all about!'

'But how?'

'That's why we're down here. I've got a plan. A really daring plan, if you're up for it!'

Charlie frowned even more. 'Go on . . .'

'I'm going to try and meet up with Jack. I'm going to ask him what he's up to.'

Charlie gulped. 'Where are you . . .?'

Zak interrupted abruptly. 'Here! And before you ask "when" . . . right now!'

Charlie almost fell out of his chair. 'But . . . but . . . how?'

Zak reached into his bag and took out two candles and a pair of matching wooden candlestick holders. 'Mum let me borrow these. I said they'd help me with my writing – fire my imagination – more atmosphere.'

'Come off it! Your imagination's fired up enough already!'

'That's what Mum said.'

'So why the candles?'

'I don't know. I just thought they might help. They make things spooky.'

'You mean they attract ghosts?' Charlie said nervously.

Zak nodded.

Charlie watched with interest as Zak placed the candles in their holders and lit them. He put one candle on his desk under the window and the other at the far end of the shed on a shelf. It was only just starting to get dark, but when Zak flicked off the light switch the candles flickered with dramatic effect. Shadows quickly invaded the shed walls giving an instant eerie atmosphere.

'Wow!' Charlie gasped. 'Spooky!'

'Yep . . . just the way I want it.'

'So now what do we do?' Charlie asked, his spectacles reflecting the candlelight.

'We wait and hope,' Zak said mysteriously.

'Wait and hope for what?'

'We wait for Jack. And we hope that I can make contact with him.'

Charlie's specs bobbed up and down as he screwed his nose up. 'You really think he'll appear?'

Zak nodded solemnly. 'I think there's a good chance he'll

appear, *to me*, and that animal will be the first to know he's on his way.' He pointed down at Killroy. The cat seemed to hear him and opened one eye.

'Twice Jack has knocked on the walls of this shed; I know it was him. And twice I've fled out of here. But not this time! This time I'm staying put.'

Charlie gulped. 'Are you sure about this?'

'As sure as my name's Zak Freeman!'

'Zak Madman! That's what you should be called!' Charlie laughed nervously.

'Ssshhh,' Zak suddenly whispered. 'Can you hear something?'

They both looked instinctively towards the window. It had turned much darker. The candle on Zak's desk reflected in the glass, making it impossible to see outside.

'Yes . . .' Charlie whispered back. 'I can hear some sort of light tapping sound.'

Zak nodded. He could hear it too. And then lots of light taps sounded on the window. He shot round and looked down at the cat; Killroy had both eyes open now, but still lay curled up.

'I'll sneak over to the door and have a peep outside,' Zak said bravely. He picked up a torch from a shelf underneath his printer and got up from his seat.

Charlie gripped the arms of the armchair and nodded stiffly. 'Good luck!'

The sinister tapping sounds increased . . . louder and more frequent . . . all over the window.

'OK . . . here goes nothing!' Zak tried to sound brave. In truth, he'd never felt more nervous. He flung the shed door open and leapt outside, aiming his torch beam in front of the window. He shrieked out in amazement.

'WHAT . . . WHAT IS IT?' Charlie called out nervously from inside the shed.

'JUST GET OUT HERE!' Zak called back. 'THIS IS DOUBLE "A" MAZING!'

12

Ghostly Meeting

Zak and Charlie stood side by side, entranced by the blizzard. The garden was already painted white and a pale light had softened the blunt blackness of the night sky.

Zak gasped, his face stinging under the hail of snowflakes. 'Incredible!'

'Triple "A" mazing!' Charlie beamed. He shook his head and a layer of snow fell off his glasses.

'Are you two OK?' a familiar voice sounded from up at the house.

Zak squinted through the driving snow and made out the figure of his father calling from the back door. 'Yep! We're fine. We'll stay down here a bit longer.'

'Well get back inside! You'll catch your deaths!'

Zak and Charlie dashed back inside the shed. The warm air hit them; Killroy was pacing around by the heater.

'Not even a ghost would come out on a night like this!' Charlie smirked.

Zak made sure the door was firmly closed and sat back down in his swivel chair. Charlie plonked himself down in the armchair. One of the candles flickered and Killroy let out a loud meow. Zak looked straight to the other candle – it flickered a little too. Killroy whined.

'Something's happening,' Zak whispered. 'Can you feel it?'

Charlie had taken a tissue out of his pocket and was wiping the lenses of his glasses. 'Yes . . . it's snowing. That's all.'

Killroy trotted over and rubbed his body along Zak's ankles.

'You sense it too, boy, don't you?'

Both candles were flickering in unison now. The shadows of the two boys shimmered in sinister fashion on the shed walls. The cat jumped up onto Zak's desk, arched his back and peered nervously towards the snow-covered window.

KNOCK! KNOCK! KNOCK!

Killroy hissed.

'Oh blimey!' Zak gasped.

'What's wrong?' Charlie asked.

'The knocking! He's here!'

Charlie looked confused. 'What knocking?'

'You didn't hear it?'

Charlie shook his head.

Zak swivelled round in his chair to face the back wall.

KNOCK! KNOCK! KNOCK!

'It's . . . it's definitely him!' Zak stammered. 'He's here!'

'You're trying to wind me up!' Charlie sighed.

Zak kept quite still and stared at the shed wall. Killroy stared too, all the fur on his back standing on end.

'Well? Now what?' Charlie asked, looking very bemused.

'We wait!' Zak replied.

Killroy ran over to the door and clawed at it, hissing and spitting. Zak opened it a little and let him out. 'Jack's close . . . very close!'

Charlie stood up and shivered. 'It's gone really cold in here.'

Zak beckoned him to sit down. 'I've got an idea.'

Charlie sat down and frowned. 'Go on.'

Zak stood to attention, his gaze firmly fixed on the back wall. 'IF YOU'RE THERE, JACK . . . KNOCK TWICE!'

The two boys stared at each other, both waiting with bated breath.

KNOCK! KNOCK!

'He's replied,' Zak gasped.

'I still didn't hear anything,' Charlie whispered.

'DO YOU KNOW WHO I AM?' Zak shouted. 'IF YOU DO . . . KNOCK ONCE!'

The candles flickered so wildly that Zak feared they were going to go out.

KNOCK!

'Yes . . . he's knocked again.'

'Let me try,' Charlie suggested. 'If I can't hear him . . . maybe he can hear me!'

'OK,' Zak nodded. 'Give it a go.'

'DO YOU KNOW WHO I AM?' Charlie called out. 'IF YOU DO . . . KNOCK ONCE!'

Zak stared at Charlie. They both waited. After a few tense seconds, Zak shook his head. 'No . . . nothing!'

Charlie looked slightly more relaxed. 'It's obvious I'm not a part of this,' he whispered.

Zak's stomach fluttered wildly. 'OK! So I'm the only one who can contact him! Right . . . here goes . . .' He took a deep breath. 'WILL YOU SHOW YOURSELF? KNOCK TWICE FOR YES!'

The words had hardly left Zak's lips when both candles went out, plunging the shed into darkness.

'What's happening?' Charlie gasped.

Zak groped for the light switch, flicked it on. Nothing happened. 'The power's gone off!'

Charlie jumped up and leaned over Zak's desk towards the window. 'Do you think he's out there?'

Zak strained his eyes, trying to see though the window. The snow was still falling fast, driving up against the glass. 'Can't see much . . .' He leaned closer, his nose almost touching the pane.

A ghostly face appeared on the other side of the glass. Big mournful eyes staring in at him.

Zak shrieked and fell backwards.

'What's up?' Charlie yelled.

Before Zak could answer, the light came back on and the shed door swung open. It banged heavily against the wall, a shower of snow falling onto the floor.

Charlie rushed over and slammed the door shut again. Zak's eyes shot back to the glass – the face was gone.

'OK . . . that's it . . . I'm going outside!' Zak announced. He braced himself, stood tall – like a soldier about to go into battle, and advanced towards the door. He flung it open and stepped outside.

'Are you sure about this?' Charlie called after him.

'Yes – I've got to find Jack!' Zak called back. His feet padded on the freshly fallen snow as he took a few steps and scanned around. He stopped dead in his tracks . . .

Jack was there – right in front of him – standing in the centre of the snow-covered garden.

The pale figure stood as still as a statue, staring forward with a frightened expression. Zak found himself standing in exactly the same way. He suddenly imagined he was a gunfighter, hands on his guns, ready for a shooting match.

'WHAT DO YOU WANT?' he called through the snow.

The boy swivelled and pointed towards the neighbour's house.

Zak didn't understand. 'MRS B LIVES THERE! WHAT ABOUT IT?'

The boy's mouth opened wide . . . trying to say something. But again there was no sound. Zak tried to read his lips.

. . . Two words. The first word was an 'S' word and the second an 'O' word. That was all he managed to pick up. He swallowed hard and stepped towards the boy.

Charlie's voice called from somewhere behind. 'ARE YOU OK? CAN YOU SEE ANYTHING?'

'IT'S OK, CHARLIE! JUST STAY WHERE YOU ARE!' Zak called back. He took another step towards Jack. The ghost-boy shimmered like a spectral snowman. He continued to mouth the two words and then held up his hands showing six fingers.

Zak twigged the 'S' word immediately. He shouted through the veil of snowflakes, 'SIX!'

The ghost-boy nodded and pointed back at Mrs B's.

Suddenly it all made sense. 'YOU WANT TO MEET ME AT SIX O'CLOCK AT THE HOUSE NEXT DOOR!'

The ghostly head nodded slowly.

'WHEN?' Zak shouted. 'TOMORROW . . . AFTER SCHOOL?'

The boy shook his head. He closed his eyes, leaned his head on his hands as if asleep and then 'woke up' again.

'IN THE MORNING?' Zak gasped. 'SIX O'CLOCK TOMORROW MORNING!'

The ghost-boy nodded and faded away.

Zak was left speechless. He couldn't believe what had just happened.

I've actually communicated with a ghost.

He felt elated and frightened at the same time. And then he remembered Charlie back in the shed. He picked up a snowball, turned and threw it at the shed window. It hit the glass with a heavy thud.

Charlie came hurtling out and dashed towards him. 'God! What happened?'

Zak brushed the snow off the top of his head and pointed towards where the ghost-boy had been standing. 'He was there! He tried to speak to me. I had to read his lips . . . and he made some signs.'

'Wow!' Charlie gasped. 'I was watching you all the time and I never saw anybody.'

'He wants to meet up at six in the morning.'

'Blimey, that's early.'

The two friends trudged through the snow towards the house. Zak looked at the footprints behind them. And then he looked to where the ghost-boy had stood. *No footprints!* He pointed over the garden wall towards Mrs B's. 'That's where he wants to meet.'

'YOU TWO! GET IN HERE!'

'OK, Dad! Coming!' Zak called back. He looked at Charlie – his glasses were almost snowed over again. 'You really didn't see him, did you?'

'Nope, not a thing.'

Charlie's mum appeared at the door. 'Charlie, come and get ready! We need to get off before we get snowed in.'

Zak took a last look up and down the garden. The snow was coming down thicker than ever. Their footprints had already covered over. It was like nothing had ever happened – all in Zak's mind, as his parents would have said.

And then he glanced back to Charlie's face – he looked really scared. These events were *real*! And like it or not, Zak sensed he was involved in something sinister and dangerous.

13

Yesteryears

Zak hardly slept. His mind was racing. He tossed and turned, constantly glancing at the electronic display on his bedside clock. Finally, he drifted off to sleep. And then, all too soon, the beeping alarm startled him back to wakefulness.

The time had arrived! Jack would be waiting for him.

Zak almost jumped out of his skin as a loud rapping sounded on the bedroom window. He peered out through the curtains . . . no one there. He wondered if it was a signal from Jack.

But how could Jack reach the bedroom window? Zak asked himself.

He eased himself out of bed and slipped into his clothes, neatly arranged in readiness for a quick exit. This included an extra sweater and two pairs of socks – he guessed the snow would be deep outside. He remembered the St Christopher on his bedside cabinet; he slid it into his pocket, and moved out onto the landing – everything seemed quiet – just the sound of Dad snoring.

He crept slowly downstairs. Everything was still in darkness.

Creeping across the kitchen he took a quick sip of orange juice from a bottle in the fridge and munched on a chocolate digestive from the biscuit barrel. That was breakfast done! His big boots were waiting by the radiator at the side of the door – they felt reassuringly warm as he slid his feet into them. Finally, on with a thick hoodie . . . and he was ready.

Holding his breath, he turned the back door key and eased the door open. He braced himself for the icy blast and stepped outside. Sure enough, it was freezing cold. But no snow – everything clear!

Zak couldn't understand it. *What's going on?*

He pulled the door shut and made his way to the passage; everything seemed somehow darker and different. He made his way quietly down the passageway – there was no iron gate at the other end – just an open space.

Zak's mind reeled in confusion.

At the front of the house he stood under the light of the streetlamp; it was different to the one that usually stood there. This one was old-fashioned, like those Zak had seen in period film sets: Sherlock Holmes, that sort of thing! There was also a strong smell of smoke. It hung heavy in the early-morning air and caused him to cough. He looked down the street and saw that all the chimneys were smoking and there were dim lights in the windows. The 'For Sale' and 'To Let' signs that had frequented many of the houses had disappeared. And then he saw that the entire street was cobbled, like the passageway.

Zak started to panic. *I can't get my head around this!*

He tried to keep calm. He studied his watch under the lamplight – almost six a.m. It was time to look for Jack the Ghost-Boy. He said he would be next door, *but where exactly?*

'Did . . . did 'e get yer up?'

The words sounded in Zak's head. His heart skipped a beat. He reeled round and saw Jack standing on the front doorstep of Mrs B's. Although only a few metres away his pale figure looked blurry and distant.

'Did who get me up?' Zak asked in amazement.

'Knocker-up man?'

Jack's voice trembled with nervousness. But Zak didn't have a clue what he was on about. 'Who?'

Jack's ghostly figure pointed across the road. A man carrying a long pole was working his way up the other side of the street, tapping the end of his pole on the upstairs windows of the houses as he walked past.

''E always goes down our side and back up t'other side. 'E makes sure we're all up in time to get t'mill.'

Zak nodded solemnly. 'Yes . . . he nearly gave me a heart attack . . . just like you've done a few times!'

Jack smiled a ghostly smile and held out a ghostly hand. 'I'm sorry if I've frightened yer. I 'ad to be sure yer was right one to 'elp me. I know I must 'ave scared yer, standing there at the end of yer bed, but I wanted to talk to yer on yer own. I was just as scared meself . . . that's why I couldn't speak to yer.'

Zak felt strangely calm. He stepped towards Jack and saw at once that the ghost-boy was truly a ghost. He could see straight through him to Mrs B's front door – though the door was different. No longer the peeling green paint, now just bare wood, dull and weather-beaten.

Zak moved closer. Jack's face looked as scary as ever, but the eyes were less fearful, more pleading and vulnerable. The ghostly mouth moved again, the cherry-red lips sending more words into Zak's head.

'I want yer to come with me. Take my hand.'

Zak reached out. As he touched the ghostly hand, a sharp tingling sensation ran through his fingers. It rose up his arm and spread throughout his entire body. The tingling quickly turned to a warm glow and Zak felt reassured – more at ease than he'd ever felt before.

Wow! I can't believe this is happening!

More words formed in Zak's head.

'Now yer invisible, like me.'

Zak looked himself up and down. His body had become like Jack's – sort of 'see through'. He could see the paving slabs through his feet. It was all so weird.

'What are we going to do?'

'I'm taking yer to Greenlands. I want to show yer where it all 'appened.'

'What do you mean?'

Jack's eyes grew wide with fear again.

'Come with me. Yer'll see for yerself.'

A distant piercing wail reached Zak's ears. At the same time the front doors of the houses opened and a host of shadowy figures spilled out onto the street. Jack led Zak to join them.

They were soon marching on amongst the strange gathering procession.

'Who are these people?' Zak asked his companion.

'Mill workers.'

Zak gawped at the groups of darkly dressed women wearing shawls over their heads and shoulders; they moved quickly down the street, heads down, talking to each other in low whispers. Men wearing wide-brimmed flat caps mingled among them. Children tagged on behind, quiet and sullen – dressed in similar fashion – miniatures of their parents.

There was a deafening sound of feet on cobbles.

Jack saw the look on Zak's face. 'It's our wooden clogs. We all wear 'em. Yer can tell the weather by the sound they make.'

Zak glanced down at Jack's rough wooden shoes. 'I don't know what you mean.'

'Quiet feet mean heavy snow . . . it deadens the sound.'

Zak put his hands to his ears. 'And what about loud feet?'

'"Ringing" we call it! And that means frost.'

Zak looked down. Sure enough the cobbles glistened under a thin white coat.

'But your shoes are special,' Jack added, 'like mine. They won't ever make a sound. Ghost's shoes, see! Come on, follow me!'

Zak walked on and stared down at his feet. His big boots made no sound on the cobbles – like he was walking on air – drifting through the crowd, nobody giving him a second look. He began to feel giddy – like he was trapped in a strange dream.

As they reached the end of School Street and turned the

corner, Zak saw that the traffic lights and busy main road were no longer there. It was a narrow lane with more and more people joining the throng and marching along it.

Suddenly, in the distance, over the heads of the crowd, Zak recognised a chimney with smoke pouring out of it – it was tall and round with a square bit at the top: the mill chimney.

The piercing siren wailed again and the mass of workers surged forward. Zak lost sight of Jack, but almost as quickly spotted him again; he was turning with the crowd down the track to the river, heading on towards the mill yard.

Ignoring the countless shadowy figures, Zak sprinted forward. He felt really safe – like nothing could hurt him. After all, he couldn't feel anything – not the floor, not the crowd, not even the cold morning air. He truly felt like a ghost!

He finally caught up with Jack at the entrance to the mill yard, standing by the side of the huge iron gates. The torrent of mill workers surged through them heading towards the mill buildings.

Jack stretched out his hand again. Without hesitation Zak took it and the two young phantoms shot high into the air. Zak clenched his teeth and screeched at the same time. 'Wowwwweeeeeee . . .!'

Up and up they went, soaring over the roof of the mill towards the chimney. When they reached the side of the tall brick structure, they shot up the side of it – higher and higher. For Zak it was the most breathtaking experience ever – like some futuristic fairground ride. He hardly dared look down. When they reached the square opening at the top, the chimney had stopped smoking. Jack dropped into a sitting position on its wide brick rim, his legs dangling casually over the side. He pulled Zak down by the side of him and pointed all around.

Zak's eyes opened wide as he took in the incredible view.

Down below, the dirty-brown river wound its way through the valley and away into the distance. The fields bordering the river looked pale and grey. In fact, everything below looked grey, including the sea of heads still making its way from the grim houses on the lower slopes of the valley to the sombre mill buildings beneath them.

Zak guessed why Jack had brought him here.

The smog and pollution that hugged the valley bottom was no doubt the curse of the people's lives. But up here, things looked different. The sun was breaking in the east and from their dizzy perch he saw that the higher slopes of the valley looked radiant and beautiful – greener than green and cleaner than clean. Above their heads, higher still, birds spiralled in the clear blue sky, revelling in the early morning sunshine. Zak turned to Jack and watched him gazing up at them. For the first time, he saw that Jack was smiling . . . a scary spooky smile, but a smile all the same.

The ghost-boy turned his attention back to Zak, his eyes filling with fear again. 'Time to go . . . we're going down!'

Zak knew instinctively that their few moments of pleasure were over. Jack was pointing down to the sloping roof of the mill. They were going into the workplace . . . to the place where Jack had no doubt met his grim end.

Zak gripped Jack's slender hand, and the two of them drifted downwards.

'Whoooooohhhhhh!'

They fell like two parachutists . . . down and down towards the grey-slated roof of Greenlands Mill.

14

Jack Attack

Down and down they dropped. The chimney was so tall it seemed to take an eternity. On reaching the roof, Zak instinctively tensed, stiffened his ankles and braced himself for the collision. Nothing happened . . . they passed straight through it. It was too much . . . too incredible. Zak closed his eyes, convinced he was dreaming. When he opened his eyes again, he was standing inside a room surrounded by a number of women sitting on wooden stools. The room had a strange smell – a dry fusty smell. Each of the women had a large sack between their knees; they were sifting through the sacks as if they were looking for something.

'Wool pickers!' Jack said from beside him.

Zak nodded. He watched the nearest woman take a handful

of wool and begin picking through it. She put the 'picked' wool into a basket by her side and threw the bits into another basket. The other women were doing the same. The room was full of dust – some of the women coughed loudly.

'Looks boring!' Zak said.

'It is. And the pay's not much good either. Some of the women pick wool all day and again when they get home. They 'ave to. They need the money.'

Zak stared around at the 'pickers'. They looked grubby, their clothes dirty and their hair greasy and dishevelled. One of the women looked younger than the others – her hair had no grey in it. She had a red mark on the side of her face. 'Wonder what happened to her?' Zak whispered.

Jack's face looked drawn and his voice trembled in Zak's head. 'She's the new lass. She answered him back. 'E slapped 'er good 'n' proper!'

Zak turned towards Jack . . . saw the fear in his eyes. 'Who did?'

Jack's ghostly voice faltered again. 'Bill . . . Bill Murdoch!'

A shiver rattled down Zak's spine. Before he could say anything else, Jack grabbed his arm and the two of them drifted over to the far side of the room. They faced a double sliding door. It was closed and the whirring of heavy machinery sounded from the other side. Jack drifted through the door, pulling Zak with him. Zak closed his eyes and braced himself again. His body passed straight through the door. He opened his eyes and recognised the room immediately.

The torture room . . .

This room had a distinct greasy, oily smell. In front of them, a set of huge metal rollers rotated slowly. The rollers were stacked on top of each other and studded with metal spikes. Two men stood in front of the machine, feeding lengths of matted wool into the rollers.

'This is the carding room,' Jack said, his voice a little calmer.

'What's it do?' Zak asked, still thinking about Bill Murdoch.

'Those spikes comb the wool into long strands ready for spinning. See 'ow they stretch it out.'

Zak watched in fascination as a length of wool disappeared between the metal rollers. It reappeared stretched out along the metal spikes of another roller and disappeared again. Finally, it emerged from the back of the machine in long drawn-out strands and dropped into a waiting basket. The rollers turned and 'clonked' ominously.

'That machine is awesome. But I wouldn't like to fall into it.'

'A man once did,' Jack sighed. 'At least 'is arm did. 'E 'eld on to the wool too long and got 'is 'and stuck. Pulled his arm straight out of the socket. By the time 'is arm got to the other end . . .'

'OK! I've got the picture!' Zak interrupted. 'Like I said to my mate Charlie, it looks more like a torture instrument!'

Zak stared around the room. Apart from the huge machine, there were just some bales of coarse wool tied up in a corner with a tangle of old string by their side. The room was full of dust, and really noisy from the whirring of the machine. The conditions in here were even worse than in the previous room. The men working the machine didn't speak to each other. One of them had a black eye.

'Don't tell me!' Zak said, staring towards him. 'Bill Murdoch!'

Jack nodded. ''S right! 'E's always hitting out at folk. Everybody's afeared of 'im. Come on, let's go and see Jenny.'

Zak's mind went back to the meeting with The Ferret: *he'd mentioned 'Jenny' – something about a 'mean machine'?* And then he remembered the conversation with Mrs Hardwick, the school librarian. She'd talked about the Spinning Jenny – the loom. It was beginning to make sense.

Jack led Zak across the room to face another double sliding door. The noise from the other side was almost deafening. The two boys passed through the metal doors and this time Zak didn't even close his eyes. On the other side Zak gawped at the sight before them.

This room was huge, bigger than the assembly hall at Zak's school. There was an even stronger smell of oil and grease and dust clouds everywhere. Workers scurried around the room watching over long lines of threads spinning between two funny cone-shaped things . . .

'They're the bobbin pins. The wool winds off them on the far side of the room and stretches and twists onto the ones at t'other end. It's called "spinning" and this machine is called a loom. It's known as a "Spinning Jenny".'

Jack's voice, though still sounding in Zak's head, was drowned out by the deafening noise of the loom. Zak had to stare at Jack's mouth to help him pick out the words. It was the same for the workers; they weren't speaking to each other. They were making signs – communicating with the use of their hands and fingers. A man made a sign to a woman and she rushed over to one of the long lines of thread. It had broken and she began tying it back together.

'That woman's a "tier" and that's Joseph scurrying around underneath 'er.'

As Jack pointed, Zak spotted a boy scratching around the floor. The loom continued spinning close above his head.

'Isn't that dangerous? What's he doing?'

'It's what I used to do. 'E's picking up all the bits of wool from the floor, collecting it, like. Nowt's wasted. It'll all be used again.'

Zak's mind went back to the meeting with the Ferret. 'Don't tell me . . . he's a scavenger.'

Jack's eyes opened even wider than usual. 'You're right! 'Ow did yer know?'

'I know more than you think.'

Zak started counting the long lines of spinning threads: *one, two, three* . . .

He lost count when he got to *thirty-four* and he was still only halfway up the huge room. It really was an incredible sight. *All that wool . . . all that spinning!*

Dozens and dozens of workers busied themselves around the machine – women tying broken threads, strong well-built men carrying bulky baskets filled with bobbin pins or freshly spun yarn. All of their faces looked pale . . . drawn. Many of them were coughing badly. Some of the older workers looked distinctly ill. The children looked pale too . . . like the faces Zak had seen in the school playground. They stood around the edge of the room waiting for a chance to dart under the machinery and 'scavenge' up the scraps of wool.

Jack suddenly clung tight onto Zak's arm. ''E'll be coming soon . . . I want yer to see what 'e's like.'

Zak's heart skipped a beat. He knew exactly whom Jack was talking about.

Over on Zak's left, by a grimy window, two men were winding carded wool onto pins ready for spinning. A nearby thread broke and one of the men made signs to a girl standing over on Zak's right. The girl was coughing badly, her lungs no doubt full of dust, but she made her way over. Instead of tying the thread she began signing to the two men. A boy took the opportunity to scurry across with a small basket and disappear beneath the loom.

'Look yonder! Look yonder!' Jack suddenly cried out. He clung to Zak's arm even tighter.

Zak looked to the far end of the room and saw a woman frantically tapping the side of her head with two fingers. She was mouthing words at the same time and although Zak couldn't lip-read, he could easily tell what she was saying:

'He's coming! He's coming!'

She continued frantically tapping the side of her head – desperate to warn everyone – just as Mrs Hardwick, the school librarian, had explained.

As the workers picked up the warning, the atmosphere in the room changed dramatically. Some of the loom operators kept their heads down and stared hard at the machinery. Others moved around staring intently at the spinning threads, willing them to break, giving them reason to be busy. The children disappeared like rats beneath the great spinning loom – safer under there than in the presence of *him*.

Jack began to shake. His form paled and shimmered and he became more blurry, more ghostlike, like he was about to disappear. He pointed to the girl and the two men, still signing to each other by the window. They were the only ones in the workspace not to have seen the warning.

Zak swallowed hard as the woman signing the warning gave up and ran over to a broken thread; she began tying it. At the same time, a single door in the far corner of the room thrust open and an imposing figure stood in its entrance.

Even from where Zak was standing, the distant figure looked huge and threatening. It was as broad as it was tall and took up most of the doorway.

Jack cowered backwards, as if the big man could see him. 'That's 'im!' he gasped from Zak's side. ''E's 'ere . . . the Overlooker . . . Murdoch! And by the look of 'im 'e's been drinking again. 'E's . . .'e's in one of his black moods!'

15

Bully Boy

The girl and the two men were still completely unaware that the Overlooker had arrived.

Zak found himself stepping backwards as Murdoch moved out of the doorway and stormed into the room. Jack's ghostly form turned all blurry again and all but disappeared. With every approaching step the figure grew larger and more frightening. Zak stared at the face – the same horrific face he'd seen in his nightmare – big, fat and round with a twisted nose and snarling mouth. The deep-set piggy eyes were firmly fixed on the two men and the girl standing idly by the window.

'God . . . he's horrible!' Zak exclaimed.

Jack's voice trembled in Zak's head. 'He's an Overlooker. Nobody slacks off when 'e's around. Everyone's afeard of 'im.'

Whilst everyone in the room kept their heads down and pretended not to notice, the big man stomped towards the window where the girl was standing with her back turned towards him. The two men facing her suddenly saw the approaching terror and their faces turned white.

Zak gasped as Murdoch grabbed the girl's arm and spun her round. With a huge hand he fetched her a cruel blow across her head and bellowed at her to get on with her work. He pushed her with brutal force towards a broken thread and screamed at her to repair it. The two men turned away quickly and resumed their work, winding new wool onto the bobbin pins. The boy, who was scavenging below, panicked, jumped up and caught his head on the underside of the loom. Blood spurted from a cut on his forehead.

'That boy's hurt!' Zak yelled, forgetting no one could hear him.

''E won't care!' Jack said, cowering behind Zak.

At the sight of his own blood dripping onto the floor, the boy screamed. The big man looked down, spotted him and dragged him to his feet. Without any concern for his injury, he flung him towards a rough wooden bench at the edge of the room. Clutching his head, the boy stumbled and fell to the floor again. He landed in a crumpled heap. An older woman picked him up and helped him over to the bench. She sat him down and dabbed at his cut with a clean piece of rag. Murdoch cursed them both and turned away. The other workers didn't even look . . . they just carried on working. It was obvious to Zak that they were truly terrified of their Overlooker.

'That guy is one nasty piece of work!' Zak blurted out, confident that only Jack could hear him.

Jack nodded solemnly.

The big man stomped around the machinery, making a few adjustments here and there, glowering and grunting at anyone he came close to. He reminded Zak of a huge boar, snorting at the other pigs, threatening them with his every move. He drew up close to where Zak was standing and Zak saw the evil in Murdoch's deep-set eyes. He saw the perspiration glistening on his greasy skin. He could smell the stale alcohol on his breath.

And then, much to everyone's great relief, the big man strode down the length of the room and disappeared back through the door, slamming it shut behind him.

Zak breathed a sigh of relief. 'Phew! Thank God he's gone!'

'Not for long!' Jack said. ''E'll be back . . . again and again. 'E's a curse on 'em all. He makes everyone's lives miserable.' He paused and added sadly, 'Like 'e did mine!'

Zak turned and saw the haunted look on Jack's face. 'So where did *you* work?' he asked. 'Are you here somewhere? Or are you already . . .' Zak hesitated.

'. . . Dead?' Jack finished for him. 'No . . . not yet! Follow me!'

Jack rose up and drifted over the top of the loom, floating over the scores of spinning threads to the far right-hand corner of the room. Zak's ghostly form followed. He wondered where on Earth Jack was going to take him. Reaching the extreme end of the loom, Jack pointed beneath it. Zak came up beside him and stared down into a dark corner. A small boy crouched in the gloom. He was shivering with fright, still cowering from the appearance of Murdoch's bullying figure.

'Who is he?' Zak asked.

Before Jack could answer, the crouching figure looked up and Zak jumped backwards. It was Jack! Another Jack! His eyes were filled with terror. He looked pale . . . dirty.

'It's . . . it's *you*!' Zak stuttered. 'But . . . but . . . how . . .?'

'. . . How can I be in two places at once?' Jack finished for him. 'Simple!' He pointed down at the cowering figure. 'That's me when I was alive. This is me when I'm dead.'

Zak looked down at the 'other Jack' with wide eyes. 'So when did you die?'

'You mean, when was I *murdered*?'

'Y . . . yes!'

'During the strike.'

Zak's mind raced. 'When was the strike exactly?'

'Before Christmas it started. It was a Monday . . . Black Monday! I was murdered after Christmas. That was a Friday.'

'Black Friday, I suppose,' Zak added.

Jack nodded solemnly. 'Exactly! Sixteenth of January it was. And I want yer to come back 'ere with me on that very day . . . to set things straight.'

'On Black Friday?'

'Yes.'

'But . . . why me?'

'Come with me!'

Jack led Zak away. They drifted towards the outside wall . . . and passed straight through it into the cobbled yard.

Zak sighed with relief. *Phew! Fresh air! Space!*

There were few people around – just a couple of men off-loading some sacks of wool from an ancient-looking lorry. They dropped the sacks onto the floor and some other men carried them inside the building. Jack led Zak over to the far side of the yard. They sat on an old railway sleeper.

Jack looked hard into Zak's eyes. 'I picked on yer to 'elp me because of several things.'

'Like what?'

'Well, for a start, you're a lad about same age as me.'

'But there's plenty more lads . . .'

Jack interrupted. 'Like I said, that's just the start. The main thing is that yer've got a strong head. Yer believe in all this . . . yer believe it's really happening . . . yer believe in *me*!'

'And that's why you picked me?'

Jack stood up and looked down at him. 'And because you 'appened to be in the right place . . . at right time.'

Zak looked thoughtful. 'I suppose we moved into School Street around the very time when you got murdered! The sixteenth is a week on Friday, isn't it?'

'Yes . . . in your time *and* mine! It'll all come together . . . just as it should.'

A sudden thought made Zak feel uneasy. 'So on Black Friday . . . Am I supposed to stop Murdoch killing you?'

Jack's eyes suddenly took on their old haunted look. 'We've been given a chance to change things . . . to change history, like.'

Zak gulped. 'And if we don't?'

'Then I'll stay like this for ever . . . a wandering spirit . . . never at rest.'

Zak stood up and put a friendly arm around Jack's shoulder. 'I'll . . . I'll do my best . . . but I'm no superhero.'

''Ave yer got the charm I gave yer?' Jack asked.

Zak took the silver disc from his pocket and showed it to Jack.

'It didn't do much for me,' Jack sighed, 'but maybe it'll be different for you. My mother swore by it.'

Zak nodded and put it back in his pocket. The two of them sat down again.

A sharp splinter stabbed into Zak's bottom. *Ouch!*

He jumped up and rubbed the seat of his trousers, wondering why he'd suddenly felt pain. Gently sitting down again, he leaned forward and looked down at his shoes. They looked different. They were like Jack's – wooden clogs – and he couldn't see through them any more. And then he noticed the oily greasy smell on his clothes. He brought the arm of his hoodie up to his nose and saw that the sleeve was different – rough coarse material with a big leather patch on the elbow. And there was something around his neck . . . a loose scarf.

'Jack . . . what's happening?'

Now it was Jack's turn to put a supporting arm around Zak. 'Yer slipping back proper . . . into my time. This is what it'll be like on Black Friday when yer come back with me. We shan't be phantoms then. *We'll be real!*'

Zak brought his hand up to scratch his head. He was wearing a cap like Jack's . . . a wide, loose-fitting cap with a wide brim.

'This is so weird!'

He jumped to his feet, looking himself up and down, staring at his clothes, his hands, his feet . . . *I'm a scavenger*, he thought to himself.

Jack got up and put out a hand. 'I've got to go now. I'll see yer a week on Friday. Same time and place as we met afore.'

Zak shook Jack's hand. 'What about me? What happens now?'

'Count to twenty. When you get to twenty you'll wake up in bed . . . back in your own time. Trust me!'

A different voice suddenly interrupted their conversation.

'SO THAT'S WHERE YER HIDING!'

Zak froze. He knew that voice. He stood to attention, arms rigid by his side, staring across the yard at the sinister figure.

'YER NOWT BUT LAZY BRATS! I'LL FLAY YER ALIVE!'

Zak stood frozen . . . like a rabbit caught in a car headlight . . . his brain trying to work out whether he was still a ghost or not.

The big man set off across the yard, his fists clenched by his sides. Jack was already away, sprinting like a greyhound. He shouted back over his shoulder. ''URRY UP AND COUNT TO TWENTY LIKE I TOLD YER!'

Zak panicked. He didn't know whether to count or run. He instinctively turned to run and stumbled over the railway sleeper. He scrambled to his feet and ran towards the big iron gates at the entrance to the yard.

'DON'T YE DARE RUN AWAY FROM ME. WHEN AH CATCH YE AH'LL . . .'

Zak sprinted for his life out through the gates and into the lane, never once daring to look back. The millstream gurgled by his side, running fast and clear. His mind went back to his nightmare, when the water had run blood red.

He tried to focus his mind and began counting, at the same time running on like a frightened rabbit. 'One . . . two . . . three . . .' His heart was bursting . . . the deep threatening voice growing louder behind him. '. . . nine . . . ten . . . eleven . . .' Murdoch was a big man, but he could still move fast. '. . .

thirteen . . . fourteen . . . fifteen . . .' Zak stopped and turned. Murdoch was almost upon him. '. . . seventeen . . . eighteen . . . nineteen . . .' He gasped in horror as the big man leapt towards him, fists clenched and evil in his eyes. 'NOW YIR FOR IT!'

'. . . TWENTY!'

Murdoch grabbed him by the shoulder and took a swipe at his face.

Zak screamed in pain – and all went black.

16

Searching the Net

Zak woke up with a start and sat bolt upright in bed. He stared around his bedroom, his mind reeling. Everything was in darkness . . . eerily silent after the deafening noise and all the goings-on at the mill.

Had it all been a dream . . . a nightmare?

The pain from his left cheek told him different. He rubbed his face where Murdoch had slapped him, easing the stinging sensation. He lay back down again, his head sinking into the pillow. He started going over all that had happened, trying to make sense of it.

One thing was for sure: the whole frightening experience had *not* been a dream. Everything had happened just as Jack had shown him. OK, so it had happened a long time ago.

But for some reason the past and the present seemed to be merging together.

He sat up and looked on his bedside cabinet . . . the St Christopher was still there . . . as if it had never been moved. He reached into the drawer and took out a notebook and pencil. He recalled the advice the author had given on his visit to the school:

'Always keep a notebook by your bed. If you have any good ideas during the night – maybe in a dream, or a nightmare – make a note of it straight away. If you don't, you'll more than likely forget it by the morning.'

Well, this was much more than a dream or a nightmare. And as Zak felt wide-awake, he decided to write things down whilst they were fresh in his mind. He could always transfer things later into his PC journal.

He leant back in bed, propped himself up onto his pillows and tried to work out the date. At first, he wasn't even sure what day it was.

Mmm . . . Wednesday . . .

It took Zak a while to work out the date, but he finally arrived at the 7th January.

That means it's the 9th on Friday. A week on Friday will be the 16th . . . same as Jack said, Black Friday!

A sudden thought brought butterflies into Zak's stomach. He began to write:

Dreams and Nightmares
Just when I think things can't get any weirder . . . they get weirder! I won't be telling Mum and Dad about my night-time journey. They already think I'm losing it. I'm

*getting so wrapped up in all this ghostly stuff, I think
I'm beginning to turn into a ghost myself. I really did
turn into a ghost this morning – or was it last night?
And then, just before Jack left me, I turned into a mill
worker – a scavenger – just for a time. I know now
how he felt, with that bullying Murdoch hounding
him. Murdoch is the most terrifying guy I've ever come
across – he's scarier than Dracula, Frankenstein's monster
and The Hulk all rolled into one. I'll never forget him
chasing me. And the way he grabbed me and slapped me
with his giant hand. My face is still stinging!*

*It seems I'm going to meet up with Jack again. He
said it would be on Black Friday. I've just worked out
that the date of Jack's Black Friday matches the date of
a week next Friday, 16th January. It seems the past and
present really are merging together! It seems we're going
to team up and try and change things . . . change history
maybe. Nobody would ever believe that! Except for one
person . . . Charlie Mann. I'm going to see him at the
weekend . . . get his advice. It'll be good to see Charlie's
cheery face again.*

ZF

Zak yawned. A little light filtered in through the curtains. It
would soon be time to get up. He yawned again and closed
the notebook, placing it on the bedside cabinet with the
pencil. He lay back and let his head sink deep into his pillow.
He tried to shut everything out of his mind – he needed sleep
– proper sleep. A short while later, he drifted off and started
snoring. He snored so loud he woke his mother across the

landing. She smiled to herself, turned over and went back to sleep.

It was only then that a more sinister sound arose from somewhere deep in the house. No one heard it. It came from downstairs . . . from the bottom of the cellar steps . . . a faint chopping sound. *Chop! Chop! Chop!*

*

Saturday couldn't come quick enough. It took two buses to get to Charlie's house. But Zak didn't mind. He needed to get away – talk things through – get Charlie's slant on things. And now they were sprawled across Charlie's bed, laid back with their hands behind their heads, staring up at the ceiling.

'If I hadn't seen some of those weird things myself, I'd say you were crackers,' Charlie said seriously.

Zak stared up at the light bulb. He closed his eyes and counted how long he could still see the light. 'I know. It all sounds crazy.'

'And you think you're going to link up with him again.'

'Yes . . . next Friday.'

Charlie sat up and brought his knees up to his chest. 'Why then?'

Zak sat up in the same way. 'It's exactly the same date as he got murdered. Black Friday! I think he's going to show me what happened.'

Charlie turned and stared at him. As usual, his eyes looked huge behind his glasses. 'He wants you for a witness. He's going to prove to you that Murdoch did it.'

Zak shook his head. 'I don't think so. What good would

that do? It's not like I could get him arrested, is it? Murdoch must have died years ago.'

Charlie jumped off the bed, went over to his computer and switched it on. 'So what's the point then?'

Zak looked thoughtful. 'I'm not exactly sure. But I guess I'm going to find out. He said something about changing history.'

Charlie seemed preoccupied. He was sat at his computer desk and engrossed with something.

'What're you doing?' Zak asked, jumping off the bed and standing beside him.

'Searching! Look . . . I've put the name "Murdoch" in the search engine. It's brought up 258,000 entries.'

Zak pulled up a stool and sat beside his friend. 'Try narrowing the search. Type "Murdoch – Greenlands Mill".'

Charlie did as Zak suggested. He keyed the enter button and waited. Nothing of any significance came up.

'OK!' Zak said. 'Try "Jack – Greenlands Mill".'

Charlie typed it in and waited. 'Bingo! See!'

Zak looked where Charlie was pointing and read the entry:

THE SCABBAJACK STORY . . . an unsolved mystery of the Dales . . .

'Wow! Quick . . . click on it!'

Charlie pulled his chair closer to the screen and clicked on the entry. Zak edged up by his side. They waited with bated breath for the search engine to come up with the goods. A few seconds later, the text sprang onto the screen:

MYSTERY OF THE DALES – The Scabbajack Story
One of the more sinister tales handed down by Dales
folk is the story of Jack Craddock, a young boy who
disappeared under very mysterious circumstances. As a
result of enforced pay cuts, a strike started at Greenlands
Mill in Steetley. William Murdoch was an Overlooker
(supervisor) and the Union Man. But he was also a
bully, much feared by the workers and especially by the
children – they suffered terrible cruelty under his hand.
Murdoch originated from Scotland and there were
rumours that he had served a prison sentence in Glasgow
for drunkenness and violent disorder. It was he who put
the workers out on strike and defied anyone to cross the
picket line.

'This is amazing . . .' Zak said quietly. 'I can't believe we've found this . . .'

Charlie didn't reply. He was too engrossed. Zak read on:

Jack Craddock was only twelve years old. He was a 'half-
timer' spending half a day at the mill and half a day at
the local school. Like the other children at Greenlands,
he was terrified of Murdoch. Jack had a young sister.
Her name was Mary and she became seriously ill. The
Craddocks needed money for Mary's medicine and so
Jack got his family to sneak him through the picket
line. It was said that the strikers turned a blind eye
to Jack, sympathetic to his sister's needs – all except
one! It is easy to imagine Murdoch's reaction when he
found out about Jack being a scab. The story goes that

the big man spotted Jack sneaking into the mill and decided to take the law into his own hands. The boy mysteriously disappeared and neither he nor his body were ever found. There was no doubt in the workers' minds what had happened and who had carried out the evil deed. Murdoch lodged at the house of the local butcher. Rumours were rife that Murdoch had murdered Jack and chopped up his body with the butcher's own tools, dumping the young lad's remains late at night in the millstream. To this day there are those who say that on certain nights, when the moon is full, the millstream runs red from midnight 'til dawn . . . the young boy's screams ringing out into the night. There have been many reported sightings of Jack's ghost wandering by the old mill and sometimes in the village. The locals refer to the ghost as 'Scabbajack' and claim the poor soul roams the streets searching for his murderer – his heart set on justice.

As Zak read the last few words, his mind reeled with all that had happened.

He sat back stiffly on his stool, turned and stared at Charlie, his mouth wide open. Charlie stared back, equally bemused.

'So what do you reckon?' Charlie asked.

'It's . . . it's all true . . . every word of it!' Zak stammered.

'What – even the bit about the millstream running red . . .'

'I'm not saying that!' Zak interrupted. 'But all the other bits . . .' He got up, walked over to Charlie's bed and flopped onto his back. He stared up at the ceiling again.

'That last bit . . . about "searching for justice". That's what

Jack wants. Somehow, I've got to help him put things right.'

Zak stared briefly at the light bulb again, closed his eyes, saw the light still shining in the blackness. 'I think there's something else.'

Charlie walked over and sat on the edge of his bed, wiping his glasses and staring down at Zak with a curious frown. 'Go on!'

Zak stared into Charlie's big eyes. 'He wants more than revenge. He needs something else . . . something to give him peace . . . stop him being a ghost. But I don't know what it is.'

Charlie screwed up his nose. 'So . . . do you reckon you'll find out?'

Zak sat up again and stared into space. 'That's why I'm going to meet up with Jack on Black Friday. I'll go back with him, back to the time of his murder. Only this time Jack'll be ready – we'll *both* be ready – waiting for Murdoch. And then we'll see what happens.'

Zak was almost in a trance. He snapped himself out of it, turned to Charlie and saw that his friend was staring curiously at him.

'*What?*' Zak asked.

'Your hands!'

It was only then that Zak noticed he'd clenched his fists . . . really tight . . . so tight his knuckles had turned white. *Wow! I'm really hyped up for this!* he thought to himself. And then the image of Murdoch's evil face sprang into his mind. He swallowed hard as a 'fluttering' feeling invaded his stomach. He thought of Murdoch chopping Jack's body up . . . maybe soon the big man would be chopping *two* bodies up!

17

Dream Lessons

Monday morning, first period, English!

Miss Woodward walked into the room and Zak sat up straight. Not only was English his favourite lesson, Miss Woodward was already his favourite teacher. The other pupils in Zak's form liked her too. She had lots of energy, was always cheerful and passionate about writing.

'OK, my lovelies . . .'

Zak smiled. Miss Woodward was from Cornwall and he *loved* her accent.

'Today we're going to talk . . . and write . . . about our dreams.'

There was a murmur of approval from the class. Now everyone sat up straight.

Miss Woodward continued. 'But first, let me ask you a question. Why is it important to use your imagination when you're writing?'

One of the girls spoke up. 'To get ideas, Miss?'

'Yes, Rachel, you're right. But you should also use your imagination to make things seem real too. For example, when you're writing, you have to imagine that you're *actually there* . . . in your story.' The teacher closed her eyes and tilted her head back. '. . . Like you can *actually* smell . . . taste . . .' She pushed her head forward and opened her eyes really wide. '. . . And *see* what's in front of you.'

Zak glanced around. Everyone seemed impressed . . . interested. *Except for one!*

'But what if you've not got an imagination, Miss?' a boy moaned from the back of the class.

The pupils giggled. It was Henry Davenport. Henry always complained . . . about everything!

'Everyone's got an imagination, Henry. It's just that some people don't know how to use it. And that brings me back nicely to my second question.' The teacher folded her arms across her chest and looked straight at the class. 'How can your imagination work on its own, without you in control of it?'

'That's impossible, Miss!' Henry sighed.

'No it's not, Henry . . . believe me! There are times when your imagination can race along at full speed . . . take you to the most wonderful places . . . sometimes to the most terrifying places . . . and you don't seem to have any control. It's like you're not in the driving seat.' The teacher clapped her hands together. 'Come on! Think!'

For Zak, it was an easy question. He had more right to know than most. He put his hand up. 'Dreams, Miss. When you're dreaming.'

The teacher smiled at Zak. 'Exactly!'

'But I *never* have any dreams, Miss!' Henry droned.

Miss Woodward walked slowly to the back of the classroom, put her hands on her hips and looked down at Henry. 'Everyone dreams, Henry. It's a scientific fact. I had a dream last night. It was a wonderful dream. A *marvellous* dream! It was about you, Henry.'

Everyone, including Zak, swivelled round in their seat. Henry's face turned bright red.

'What happened, Miss?' one of the girls asked.

Miss Woodward closed her eyes again and clasped her hands in front of her. 'Oh, it was wonderful, Georgia. Henry was in my kitchen . . . washing a sink full of dishes.'

Henry looked up soulfully, his face still flushed. 'So what was wonderful about that, Miss?'

Miss Woodward opened her eyes and looked around at the class with a broad grin on her face. 'What was wonderful, Henry, was that you never once complained!'

The whole class burst out laughing.

'OK, everyone! You've got ten minutes to chat to the person next to you and make notes about your dreams.'

'Does that include nightmares, Miss?' one of the boys asked enthusiastically.

'Of course!' Miss Woodward replied. 'They're dreams, aren't they?'

The boy next to Zak, Hugh Morrison, started describing one of his dreams. But Zak hardly heard a word. His mind was already going over his own dreams. Nobody would ever believe how real *they* were.

The rest of the lesson passed quickly. Too quickly! Zak found it fascinating to hear what the others had to say. Some of the pupils described wonderful dreams – about things they liked. Others talked about their nightmares, describing horrors that really scared them.

At the end of the lesson, Miss Woodward said something that really made Zak sit up and take notice. 'Of course, it's worth remembering, there are those who believe dreams have a meaning.'

'Like a dream might be trying to tell you something, Miss?' Rachel Bellamy asked.

'Yes, Rachel! If you keep dreaming that you're late for an appointment and you're very upset about it, then maybe your dreams are telling you to be better organised . . . to help you in your real life.'

Jamie Cross was the class comedian. He shouted out loudly. 'Maybe your dream about Henry was telling you you'd better get a dishwasher, Miss.'

Everyone shrieked with laughter, *including Zak*. Just for a moment, he forgot all his troubles and worries. It was so good to laugh and feel normal again.

But just as the lesson ended and the pupils had packed away, his mind went back to Miss Woodward's comment:

'Of course, it's worth remembering, there are those who believe dreams have a meaning.'

The problem for Zak was that he was never quite sure whether his dreams were just dreams or whether they were really happening. Real or not, he decided that from now on, he would think about his night-time experiences very carefully.

*

Zak tucked into his breakfast feeling a little more relaxed. The last few days had passed normally – nothing untoward. He pushed another spoonful of porridge into his mouth. It was his favourite, flavoured with golden syrup. It tasted good . . . real . . . normal!

'Good to see you enjoying your food,' Zak's mum commented. 'You're looking a bit more yourself.'

Zak nodded and took another spoonful. He did feel better – no doubt about it. And then his mind went to Jack . . . Black Friday was looming up fast. A fluttering erupted in his stomach. He tried to forget about it . . . concentrate on today. He took a deep breath . . . and another spoonful of porridge.

'Glad you're feeling yourself,' Mr Freeman said from behind his paper. 'I'm away overnight and I'm leaving you and Mum in charge. You'll have to be the "man about the house".'

Zak glanced across the table. 'Where are you off to?'

'Leeds. There's a block of flats being updated not far from here. I'm having dinner with the guys in charge of the project. They're putting me up in a hotel and we'll be discussing things again tomorrow.'

'Very posh!' Mrs Freeman smiled. 'You'll have to put on your best suit.'

'Dad in a suit!' Zak chuckled cheekily. 'That'll be a sight worth seeing.'

'Well, suit or not . . . be careful on the roads,' Mrs Freeman said. 'The snow's about gone, but there's ice around. Just take your time and get there in one piece!'

Mr Freeman lowered his newspaper and looked from his wife to Zak. 'She thinks I'm still seventeen.' He chuckled. He looked back to Mrs Freeman. 'I'm old and boring now, love. There's nobody more careful than me when I'm driving.'

'Well keep it that way!' Mrs Freeman said sternly.

Zak smiled to himself. He knew how much his mum and dad cared for each other and it made him feel good . . . warm inside.

'Don't worry, Dad. We'll see to things while you're away, won't we, Mum?' Zak said in his most serious voice.

Mrs Freeman smiled. 'You bet!'

Mr Freeman buried his head behind his newspaper again. 'Good lad, Zak! Good lad!'

*

At the end of the day, Zak stayed in and watched TV. When the ten o'clock news came on, he decided to retire to bed. Mrs Freeman said she wouldn't be long after him. She said there was nothing much more on TV and she was looking forward to snuggling up in bed with her favourite book.

'OK, Mum! I'll just check all the doors are locked before I go up. Goodnight!'

'Oh . . . thanks for that! Goodnight, love! Sleep tight!'

Zak did the rounds – checked the doors, the windows, lights off in the kitchen – everything secure! After washing, undressing and getting into bed, he lay very still, listening out for Mum. A short while later, he heard her coming up the stairs. His bedroom door opened a little.

''Night, Zak,' a voice whispered from the doorway.

''Night, Mum.'

Zak lay awake . . . listening. There was still a little light coming from the direction of Mum's room. *She's still reading*, Zak thought to himself.

Finally, the faint light disappeared. All went dark.

It seemed only a short time later when Zak woke up with a start. He looked at his bedside clock – it was 3 a.m. He'd been asleep for nearly four hours.

He turned his head towards the curtains. He felt drawn towards them – he sensed there was something very weird on the other side. He slid quietly out of bed – he didn't want to wake Mum – crept over to the window and peeped out. His eyes opened wide. A cold grey light hung over the school playground. Groups of silent schoolchildren played beneath it . . . boys running and jumping . . . girls playing skipping games.

Zak had seen this scene before. But this time the ghostly children were quiet. Their mouths moved in time with their actions, but no sounds came out. The eerie silence gave the scene a sinister edge. Zak felt a chill run down his spine. He stared at a group of girls standing close by the school railings. They were holding hands in a circle and spinning round. Even from the distance, Zak could read their lips . . . tell what they were chanting:

Scabbajack . . . Scabbajack . . .

Put his body in a sack.

Zak thrust the curtains closed again and sat on the end of his bed.

Here we go again! Am I dreaming or what?

He pinched himself hard. It hurt!

This can't be a dream!

He glanced around his bedroom. Everything looked normal . . . but it didn't feel normal. The room felt heavy . . . like a weight pressing down on him. His head began to throb and a faint buzzing sound filled his ears. It was like the room was full of electricity. Something really strange was going on!

Zak took a deep breath, took his torch from his bedside cabinet and crept out onto the landing. All quiet. Mum didn't snore like Dad. He opened her bedroom door and peeped in. Even in the darkness the roomed seemed different. It had a different smell . . . an old fusty smell.

The buzzing in Zak's ears grew louder, the throbbing in his head got worse.

He switched on his big rubber torch and shone it into Mum's room. A sickening feeling welled up in his stomach. The walls had no wallpaper – just white with damp patches. The carpet had gone – just bare floorboards. The bed looked different – a brass bed head and iron legs.

Zak panicked. 'MUM!'

The room started whirling round . . . the buzzing in Zak's ears was deafening . . . the heavy atmosphere was crushing him. He moved closer to the bed and shone the torch onto the sleeping figure tucked beneath the heavy blankets.

Blankets? Zak's mum always slept under a flowery-patterned duvet!

Fear gripped Zak like never before! 'MUM! MUM!'

The sleeping figure stirred beneath the sheets. Zak aimed the powerful torch beam towards the bed head, desperate to see Mum sitting up and staring at him . . . her kind familiar eyes . . . the loving smile!

But a huge round greasy head appeared instead.

Zak gasped as Murdoch pushed back the blankets and reared up before him.

Zak stepped back and screamed . . . his ears bursting with an overpowering electrical whining sound. He bolted out of the room and shot downstairs . . . shining the torch ahead of him. Everywhere looked different – stark and run down – like it wasn't Zak's house any more.

A pounding on the ceiling above his head told him that Murdoch was out of bed. Heavy footsteps sounded down the stairs. Zak saw a half-open door in front of him. He snatched it open and dashed through it . . . *and down into the cellar!*

Oh please, no! Not the cellar!

There was no choice . . . Zak leapt down the steps three at a time. He reached the bottom. The stone table stood in front of him. A pig's head sat in a pool of fresh blood – its dead eyes seemed to stare at him. A carcass hung from one of the hooks, swinging slightly as if it had just been put there.

Gripped with terror, Zak sprinted into the fuel store. He darted into the furthest, darkest corner and hid behind an old wooden crate . . . something else that hadn't been there before! He switched off his torch and crouched in the darkness, hardly daring to breathe. A growling, grunting sound reached his ears.

A light flickered in the far cellar and Murdoch appeared carrying a candle. He held it forward, lighting up the fuel store. Zak ducked lower behind the crate, his heart racing.

'Come out, come out whoever ye are!' The voice was gruff . . . growling.

Zak didn't move a muscle.

The big man turned to the stone table and picked up a huge cleaver. With the candle in one hand, and the cleaver held high in the other, he turned back to face the fuel store.

'Break into mah house, would ye? Ah'll chop yir head off, ye wee brat!'

Zak felt dizzy. The buzzing in his ears had stopped. Now it was the silence that was overpowering. He breathed in as quietly as he could. Some coal dust got up his nose and tickled it . . . he felt a sneeze coming on!

No, please . . . don't let me sneeze!

The more he tried not to sneeze, the more his nose tickled. Murdoch took a step closer, the cleaver held menacingly above his head. Zak could smell the man's foul body odour . . . smell the stale beer on his breath.

The tickle in Zak's nose was unbearable . . . he was desperate to sneeze.

'Are ye hiding behind there?' the big man teased, stepping towards the crate.

Zak pinched his nose, but it was too late. 'ATCHOOO!'

The cleaver came crashing down, smashing into the crate, and splintering it into pieces. At the same time a huge rat shot out from the opposite corner and ran between Murdoch's giant legs. The big man shrieked and stumbled backwards. He fell onto his back and dropped the candle. The cellar was plunged into darkness.

Zak seized the opportunity and jumped to his feet. He switched his torch on and shot past Murdoch.

The big man, prostrate, but still clutching the cleaver, roared with anger. 'AH'LL KILL YE . . . AH'LL KILL YE!'

Zak was already on his way up the cellar steps, Murdoch back on his feet and after him. Two steps from reaching the kitchen, it was Zak's turn to trip. He fell headlong and dropped the torch. He put out his hands to break his fall and just managed to stop himself from smashing his face on the stone steps. Grunting and heavy breathing sounded from the cellar bottom. Zak pushed hard on the steps, desperate to get to his feet. But his left ankle was grabbed tight.

Zak swung round and saw his ultimate nightmare . . . the face of the evil murderer leering up at him. The piggy eyes . . . the bulbous nose and the leathery lips curled back into a savage snarl.

'Come here!' the man growled.

Zak screamed and tried to yank his foot free. But Murdoch held it in a vicelike grip. An agonising pain seared through Zak's ankle . . . his shin was near to breaking point.

Please let this be a dream . . . a nightmare . . . please . . . please!

Murdoch seemed to read Zak's thoughts. He laughed hysterically.

Zak could only roll over and watch helplessly as the ogre reeled him in like a fish on a line. He pulled Zak closer with one hand and raised the cleaver high with the other.

Zak closed his eyes. This was it . . . it was all over.

I'm dead meat!

18

Doctor's Orders

Zak opened his eyes. It was hard to see. It was still dark. His body was racked with pain and he shuddered with cold.

Where am I? What happened?

A voice sounded from above his head. 'What in Heaven's name?'

Zak groaned and looked up. His mother was standing at the top of the cellar steps looking down at him. He tried to smile at her . . . and then everything went black.

When he came round the second time, he felt warm and cosy. He could still feel the aches and pains, bumps and bruises, but glancing around the bed, he knew he was in a safe place.

The nurse smiled down at him. 'How are you feeling?'

Mrs Freeman stood by her side. She frowned and shook her head. 'You do cause me some worry!'

Zak snuggled under the sheets, enjoying the warmth. 'Sorry, Mum!'

'Sleepwalking can be a dangerous thing,' the nurse said, reaching for the chart on the end of Zak's bed.

'We'll tie him down from now on!' Zak's mum said sternly.

The nurse walked round to the head of the bed and peered closely into Zak's eyes. 'How do you feel? Any headaches?'

Zak shook his head.

'How many fingers am I holding up?'

'Three.'

'Mmmm . . . good!'

Zak watched as the nurse wrote something on the chart.

'What happens next?' Mrs Freeman asked.

'The doctor will need to give Zak another look over. If he gives him the all clear, you can take him home. We can give him some cream for those bruises. The ankle's sprained a little, but nothing's broken.'

At the mention of 'ankle', Zak's mind flashed back to the moment of terror . . . when the butcher had gripped him tight. His stomach churned. He looked nervously around the ward, half-expecting to see the evil man lurking in the background.

'Zak . . . are you sure you're OK?' Mrs Freeman asked, her voice full of concern. 'You've turned a funny colour.'

The nurse placed the palm of her hand across Zak's forehead. 'Mmmm . . . you feel cold and clammy.' She looked at Mrs Freeman. 'We may need to keep him overnight. We'll maybe do a few more tests just to be on the safe side. Let's see what the doctor says.'

Zak relaxed again. Staying in hospital seemed like a good idea. He really didn't feel like going home. 21 School Street was more than haunted . . . it was full of horrors! He'd had enough! He needed to think . . . get his head around everything. Staying in hospital would give him the space he needed.

'I think I do need to stay in a bit longer, Mum. I don't feel very good and my body's aching all over.'

'Like the nurse said, let's wait and see what the doctor thinks. If you do stay I can always nip home and bring you a few more things. And your dad's already on his way back from Leeds. He'll be here soon.'

Half an hour later, the doctor had given Zak the once-over and agreed that he should stay in overnight. A wave of relief washed over him. Mrs Freeman went straight home and returned with some of his belongings . . . including his sacred notebook.

'I don't know why you want that!' she'd said, handing it over with a frown. 'You need to rest that head of yours.'

'I just want to keep it up-to-date,' Zak replied.

'Well . . . I don't know what you put in there. It's none of my business, but I think it's time you gave that imagination of yours a well-earned day off.'

*

Later that afternoon, after a short nap – with no dreams or nightmares – one of the nurses propped up Zak's pillows and he began writing:

Hospital

*I'm staying in hospital until tomorrow . . . after yet
another terrifying experience. Ever since I found out
that Murdoch lived in our house, I've had this dread of
seeing his ghost again. Well it happened . . . last night!
Murdoch appeared . . . in Mum's bed!*

Zak shivered at the thought of it. The memory was too
horrible . . . he decided not to write any more on the subject.

He put his notebook and pencil on the bedside cabinet.
He laid his head back on the soft pillow and put his hands
behind his head. He stared up at the bright ceiling and tried
to concentrate. His mind went straight to Friday . . . the day
after next . . . Friday 16th January . . . Black Friday! The day
he would meet up with Jack again.

Same time, same place. That's what he said.

'You look thoughtful!'

Zak focused his attention on the young nurse standing at
the end of his bed. She picked up a clipboard and scribbled
some notes as she spoke. 'You still look pale. How do you
feel?'

Zak sat forward. 'A bit weak, but not too bad.'

'Just rest and make sure you eat plenty. It's steak pie and
chips later followed by sponge pudding. And don't forget to
drink plenty as well. You need building up.'

Zak nodded and lay back again. And then a sudden horrible
thought entered his head. Here he was . . . in hospital . . .
needing 'building up' . . . and he hadn't even met up with Jack
yet. The big test was still to come. How could he possibly be
of help to poor Jack!

I'm no good! I'm just weak and I'm a coward . . . always running away.

But then an image formed in Zak's head. It was Jack's face. He was smiling a weak feeble smile. He looked vulnerable . . . his eyes were so pleading.

The image vanished and a sense of determination suddenly surged through Zak's body. His aches and pains seemed to melt away . . . even the throbbing pain in his ankle subsided. He began to feel good . . . confident . . . not scared any more. In all the stories he'd ever read, hadn't Good always won out against Evil? So why should this be any different?

Zak sat up, reached for the notebook and pencil again, and continued where he'd left off.

I've decided not to be scared any more. I'm going to help Jack face up to that vicious bully. And when all this is over, I'll write my own story . . . and Good will beat Evil once again. And this time it will be Jack Craddock that comes out on top!

19

Time Traveller

'I still can't get over it.' Mr Freeman frowned. 'I leave you in charge with your mum for one night and you finish up laid out at the top of the cellar steps. I suppose you were beating off burglars or fighting vampires. That imagination of yours will be the death of you one day.'

Zak glanced up at his dad and smiled sheepishly.

'Don't go on at him!' Zak's mum said, placing a plate of bread on the table. 'He's been through enough. Before you go back to work, tell him about your meeting in Leeds.'

Zak sipped a spoonful of hot tomato soup and looked up at his dad with renewed interest.

'They've offered me the contract,' Mr Freeman said

proudly. 'I've got enough work lined up now to last for goodness knows how long.'

Zak reached over for a slice of thick brown bread. 'Great, Dad! That's brilliant news!'

Mrs Freeman joined them at the table. 'It is . . . but we're both a bit worried about you.'

Zak took a sip of his soup and made a loud slurping noise. 'Why?'

Mrs Freeman frowned. 'I know we've only just moved here,' she continued, 'but you've not really settled. Dad and I have discussed it . . . this house seems to have had a strange effect on you. You've got to admit it, Zak. You've been acting more than a little bit weird lately.'

'Even more weird than usual!' Mr Freeman grinned.

Zak sensed his father was trying to break the tension. 'Sorry,' Zak said over the rim of his soup spoon. 'I'll try and be a bit more normal.' He took a great bite of bread and shoved another spoonful of soup into his mouth. It tasted good. 'Dad, seeing as you got that contract, does that mean I can have more pocket money?'

His dad smiled . . . and his mum looked a little less tense!

*

Thursday passed slowly . . . too slowly! Zak was forever looking at his watch. He watched TV whilst his mum fussed around him. She'd insisted on keeping him off school and that didn't help. School always passed quickly, but sitting around at home made the time drag unbearably.

Late in the afternoon Zak phoned Charlie on his mobile.

'What time are you meeting him?' Charlie's voice crackled
– the signal wasn't brilliant.

'Six in the morning . . . like last time.'

'And you really think you can help Jack face up to
Murdoch?'

'Yep!'

'Rather you than me. That guy sounds like a serious
headcase!'

'He is . . . but me and Jack . . . we're going to sort him out
good and proper!'

There was a brief silence on the end of the Zak's phone.
'Hello! Are you still there?'

'Yep! Still here! I just can't believe that you think you've got
a chance against that ghoul.'

Zak took a deep breath and tried to put Murdoch's face out
of his mind. 'Look . . . if anything happens to me . . . tell my
mum and dad . . .'

'Let's not go there!' Charlie interrupted. 'Nothing's going
to happen to you. This is still all about dreams and stuff. I
just can't get my head around it being real. You'll be fine. A
bit brain-damaged, maybe . . . but that's nothing new!'

Zak could almost see Charlie's big brown eyes and his
freckled face beaming behind his glasses. 'So after everything
that's happened you still think this is all down to my overactive
imagination?'

There was a pause on the other end. '. . . Well, let's just
wait and see what happens.'

'Fair enough! We'll meet up this weekend – if I'm still
around – and I'll give you a full report.'

'OK, Zak . . . stay cool and good luck! Say "Hi" to Jack and

I hope the two of you give that Murdoch guy hell!'

Zak paused. He still couldn't make his mind up whether Charlie was taking him seriously or not. He couldn't really blame him if he didn't. Who would?

'Bye! See you soon . . .' He put the phone down and felt more resolved than ever. He went over to the sofa, put on his headphones and laid back. He listened to his favourite CDs one after the other. Listening to music was a sure way to relax and recharge.

Tomorrow, Zak knew he would need all the recharging he could get!

*

It was just after ten when Zak finally retired to bed. His mum made him a mug of cocoa to help him settle. It worked. Within minutes Zak was asleep. He slept deeply and could hardly believe it when his watch alarm beeped at five thirty a.m.

He sat up in bed feeling sick with excitement. *This is it . . . Black Friday!*

A short while later, he slipped out of the house. It was freezing cold. Everything looked different again. But this time, Zak was no stranger to the experience. He made his way fearlessly down the gap between the houses. As expected, Jack was waiting on the doorstep of number 25. But this time he looked different. He was no longer the shimmering see-through phantom – he was solid . . . real . . . *and he looked terrified.*

Jack held out a hand and Zak took it, expecting it to feel ice-cold like the last time. But it felt warm . . . alive!

Zak gulped. 'You're not a ghost this time!'

'No . . . and neither are yer!' Jack answered nervously. 'Yer just a time-traveller.'

Zak let go of Jack's hand; he himself felt different too . . . he even smelled different. His senses reeled as he realised he'd gone through the same change as back at the mill . . . when Murdoch had chased him. He touched all over his body . . . the wide-brimmed cap on his head, the neckerchief, the long shabby jacket, the ragged trousers and the worn-out shoes . . . he'd become a scavenger again, wearing a scavenger's clothes . . . like Jack.

He felt in his coat pockets for the St Christopher. It wasn't there. *How could it be? It was a different jacket!*

'Are yer looking for this?' Jack whispered, holding out the medal. 'Yer back in my time now . . . so the charm's back with me. Here . . . take it. Keep it safe.'

Zak slipped into his breast pocket and stooped low. His eyes darted around as he spoke to Zak in a whisper. 'Keep really quiet . . . keep yerself out of sight. The journey to Greenlands will be dangerous.'

Zak swallowed hard. 'What . . . what do you mean? Aren't you coming with me?'

'Yes, we're both going. Keep in the shadows and move as quiet as a mouse.'

The mill siren sent out its piercing sound from over the rooftops. Zak looked down the street, but this time none of the doors opened. And only a few of the chimneys were smoking.

'No time for blathering!' Jack said sternly. 'We need to move fast.'

As Jack edged past, Zak followed his course, sidling down the terraced houses, sticking to the darkest, shadowy places. At the end of School Street, an old man stood by a handcart. There were four big sacks on the cart. The man was leaning against the wall, as if waiting for someone.

'Who's that?' Zak asked, crouching low.

'Uncle Albert,' Jack replied. 'He's our helper. He'll get us through the pickets.'

Zak moved closer. Albert was wearing a broad flat cap and snow-white tufts of hair stuck out from the sides. He saw the two of them and frowned.

'What's going on 'ere, young Jack? Nobody's ever said 'owt about there being two of yer.'

''E's a friend and it's only this once!' Jack whispered.

The old man took two folded empty sacks off the cart and ushered the two boys towards him.

'Quick as tha likes, lads! Get thaselves in!'

The man's accent was so broad that Zak hardly understood. But he guessed that Uncle Albert wanted him to get into the sack – and that didn't seem like a nice idea!

'Trust 'im!' Jack's voice reassured him. 'Yer'll be safe with Uncle Albert.'

All in a flash, the old man pulled the sack down over Zak's head, tucked it around his feet and bundled him onto the cart. He did the same with Jack and arranged the other sacks around them.

'Don't thee worry, lads. Tha'll be safe with Uncle Albert.'

The cart rattled and bumped down the lane, Uncle Albert pushing it hastily towards the mill. Zak could hear his heart beating very fast. This 'adventure' was getting scarier by the minute. And this was definitely no dream! The feel of the sacking rubbing against his skin felt very real. The stink of oil and dirt on his clothes was disgustingly real. The bumping and jolting of the cart and the lack of air in the sack gave him a *real* sickly feeling.

An icy shiver ran down Zak's spine as a horrible thought entered his head. They were on their way to face Murdoch . . . *and he too would be very real!*

Showdown

As the handcart bumped over the cobbles, Zak managed to wriggle himself into a sitting position. The bottom of the cart was hard and cold . . . very uncomfortable!

Uncle Albert's voice reached his ears. 'Keep still, lads. We'll soon be at mill.'

Zak's sack had a hole in it, close to his eye. He tore at it with his fingers and made it bigger. Peeping through, he glimpsed the terraced grey houses reaching up to the leaded sky. He caught sight of a face in one of the icy windows, a woman's face. She looked suspicious and stared intently as the cart bumped and rattled on past.

A low murmur of voices sounded close, growing louder all the while. They turned a sharp corner and Zak guessed that they were on the last leg – heading down the lane towards the mill entrance.

Uncle Albert's voice confirmed his suspicions. 'Keep low, lads. We're almost there!'

Still peeping out of the hole, Zak's heart skipped a beat as he saw a large crowd of people barring the entrance to the mill gates. As the cart drew closer, he saw that they were mainly men. They stood in groups, hands deep in pockets, talking with serious faces. A fire burnt in a brazier just in front of the gates; some of the men stood by it warming their hands.

'Right then!' Albert whispered. 'Keep still and don't mek a sound.'

The cart ground to a halt. Zak peered through the hole and saw a small wiry man approach.

'Good lad, Albert! We'll need all thar wood today. It's cold enough to freeze thar breath!' Zak saw the man's face up close. His dark eyes darted around nervously. His brow was furrowed, skin blotchy and pale. 'I'll give thee a hand to off-load it.'

'No . . . I'm fine!' Uncle Albert said quickly. 'I'll stack it by the gates in the usual place.'

The man shrugged his narrow shoulders and walked away. Zak sighed with relief. Albert pushed the cart towards the big iron gates and steered over to the left-hand gatepost. Nobody challenged him. He heaved the first sack of wood off the cart and leaned it up against the stone pillar. 'All right, lads!' Uncle Albert whispered. 'Brace thaselves!'

Zak did as he was told. He curled up into a ball and tensed. Albert lifted him off the cart easily . . . the old man was still strong. He put Zak, inside his sack, alongside the first one.

'Wait 'til other sacks are beside thee, then thar can sneak through gap in't railings,' he whispered.

Zak waited. He couldn't see through the hole any more . . . the other sack had blocked his peephole. But he could hear the men on the picket line gabbling on to each other. They sounded some distance away and Zak felt reassured.

'Zak . . . are . . . are you there?' It was Jack's voice, shaking with fear. He was in the sack beside him.

'Yes . . . ready when you are.'

Albert put another sack of wood up against Zak's and was about to lift off the last sack when a horrific voice boomed out from the distance.

'IT'S REACHED MA EARS THAT SOME OF YE ARE THINKING O' GIVING UP! WELL, LISTEN TO ME AND LISTEN GOOD! THIS STRIKE WILL GO ON 'TIL WE'VE WON. DO AH MAKE MASELF CLEAR?'

Zak filled with panic. He knew that voice only too well.

Albert dumped the final sack of wood up against the two boys. 'Right, lads! Be out and away as quick as yer like. Murdoch's in a foul mood.'

Zak needed no telling. He wriggled out of the sack and crouched amongst the others. Jack did the same. They crouched side by side. Uncle Albert was already pushing the cart back towards the lane. Zak looked across and saw Murdoch standing on some sort of box by the fire. He was pouring liquid from a glass bottle into an enamel mug and swigging it. The crowd stood in front of him, listening to his booming voice.

'IF ANY ONE O' YE DARE TO CROSS THIS PICKET LINE YE'LL HAVE ME TO DEAL WITH. WE'RE NO

HAVING ANY SCABS IN THIS UNION. WE'RE HERE TO FIGHT AND WE'LL FIGHT TO THE END.'

A voice shouted back from within the crowd. 'AH'M NOT SURE YER SPEAKING FOR ALL OF US, MURDOCH. SOME OF US ARE STARVING. WE HAVE FAMILIES TO THINK ABOUT. WHAT'S THE GOOD IN FIGHTING 'TIL THE END IF WE'RE ALL DEAD ANYWAY?'

A murmur of approval rippled through the crowd. Zak tensed, waiting for the big man's reply.

Jack tugged at Zak's arm . . . pointed behind them to the railings at the side of the gatepost. One of the railings was bent slightly making a gap big enough for a boy to climb through.

Zak tensed as Murdoch's voice boomed out again.

'AH'M YOUR UNION REPRESENTATIVE . . . AND DON'T FORGET IT. LIKE I SAID . . . WE'LL FIGHT TO THE BITTER END AND IF ANYONE THINKS OTHERWISE THEY'LL HAVE ME TO ANSWER TO!'

A murmur of disapproval rippled through the crowd. The workers slunk away and stood in groups, muttering to each other in low whispers. Murdoch got down off his box, pulled it up to the brazier and sat on it, warming his huge hands. Zak saw that his face was contorted into an expression of contempt . . . no doubt contempt for his fellow workers . . . the very people he was supposed to represent.

Jack's voice trembled in Zak's ear. 'This is where it all went wrong.'

'What do you mean?'

'Black Friday. Today. He saw me sneaking in and he came after me.'

Zak swallowed hard. He'd been so preoccupied with Uncle Albert and everything else that had been happening; he'd momentarily forgotten he was here to help Jack face up to his past. Poor old Jack sounded distraught.

'Well it's not going to happen the same again. Otherwise, we won't have changed anything,' Zak said with all the confidence he could muster.

'I'm not sure we can change 'owt,' Jack said, his face turning paler by the second. 'But we can 'ave a good try, can't we?'

Murdoch's fearsome voice boomed out again. 'WE NEED MORE WOOD FOR THIS FIRE. AH'M GOING TO COOK MA MEAT.'

Zak turned towards the big man again. It was then that Zak saw the cleaver. It was stuck into a small stump of wood by Murdoch's side and it gleamed by the fire. Murdoch pulled it free and waved it menacingly in the air. The other workers stepped back. They watched nervously as the fearsome man took a package from his pocket, unwrapped it and dumped some raw meat on the stump. He turned towards the sacks of wood and gazed straight in Zak's direction.

Zak froze. He didn't know what to do. If he ran, Murdoch would see him. If he stayed put, Murdoch would find him.

Jack was already halfway through the gap in the railings. 'Quick . . . run . . . now!'

Zak jumped out from his cover and leapt towards the gap in the railings..

Murdoch saw him immediately. 'SCAB! IT'S THE SCAB! GET HIM!'

Zak glanced over his shoulder. Murdoch was running towards him. The thin, wiry man intercepted and got in the big man's way. 'Leave 'im alone. He's nowt but a lad and his sister's ailing. We all know why he's doing it.'

Some of the other men muttered in agreement.

'GER OUT OF MA WAY OR AH'LL SPLIT YIR SKULL! HE'S A SCAB AND AH'M GOING TO KILL HIM!'

At first, the thin man stood his ground and clenched his fists. Murdoch raised the cleaver and the man thought better of it . . . stepped backwards. The big man pushed him aside. At the same time Zak disappeared through the railings and sprinted after Jack across the cobbled yard.

'Where shall we go?' Zak shouted ahead.

'The sorting room! Down yon and through that door!'

Zak followed and soon found himself in a familiar place – the room where he'd seen the women sat round, picking out bits from sacks of wool. But this time, there was only one woman. She looked old and sat on her own in a corner.

'Is that yer, Jack?' the old woman asked, looking up. 'Sounds like yer've someone with you.'

Zak noted her strange eyes, blurry and colourless.

'That's Mary Malkin. She's old and she's blind.'

'Is she a scab, like us . . . er . . . I mean . . . like you?'

'Yes. But nobody bothers about Mary. Like I said . . . she's old and blind. And she's on our side. She'll help us hide . . . like before!'

'What do you mean, *like before*?'

'Like the last time . . . it's all happening again . . . just the same!'

Zak started to feel sick. 'But this time that madman's going to try to kill us *both* . . . just like he killed you?'

'Unless we can change things . . . yes!' Jack replied nervously.

The old woman spoke up. 'Come on, Jack. And your friend. Sit by me. There's a good few sacks to pick through.'

A voice boomed from outside the door. 'WHERE ARE YE? WHEN AH FIND YE . . . AH'LL SKIN YE ALIVE!'

The old woman jumped back. 'Murdoch! The devil's own! What's 'e doing 'ere?'

Jack shouted up. ''E's seen me, Mary. 'E's seen the two of us. 'E knows we're 'ere.'

'Don't fret, lads. Get behind me. Keep low and tuck yer sens 'neath the hem of my skirt.'

They did as she said. They dived behind her, lay low in the corner and pulled the hem of her skirt over themselves.

As Murdoch's huge figure burst into the room, Zak lay trembling. Beads of cold sweat formed on his forehead.

As Murdoch loomed over the old woman, his eyes ablaze with drunken rage, Zak whispered in Jack's ear. 'Will he find you? Is this where he kills you?'

Even in the darkness of the old woman's skirt, Zak could see Jack's eyes, full of torment and fear.

'No . . . not yet!' Jack sighed. 'But the time's almost upon us!'

21

The Final Curtain

'Where is the wee scab? Ah know he's in here. Where are ye hiding him?'

Zak held his breath beneath the old woman's skirts. Jack panted heavily beside him.

She replied calmly. 'My world is a world of darkness, as well yer know. So I've seen no one. But my hearing is better than most . . . and I'm telling yer, Murdoch . . . I've 'eard no one. I'm alone . . . or at least *I was!*'

'Yir a liar, Mary Malkin! Yir a soft 'un! The lad's working and earning and we're all starving out there. He's a scab and needs punishing . . . and . . . and Ah'm the man to do it!'

Zak felt his stomach tighten.

''E's a child!' the old woman snapped back. ''E's only trying to 'elp 'is sister – and where's the wrong in that? And as for yer starving, it's my guess there's meat enough in your lodgings to feed the whole village.'

Murdoch growled and spat on the floor.

Mary Malkin went on.'. . . And as for yer being the man to do *anything* . . . I'll tell yer straight, Murdoch. Yer no man! Yer a *beast*! An' a drunken beast at that! Yer supposed to be on the side of the workers . . . leading 'em out there . . . looking after their needs, but the only needs yer interested in is yer own! There's not a man or woman in this village that would give yer the time of day. They're all afeard of yer, every last one of 'em . . . in the same way folk are afeard of a wild animal. All bah me! My eyes may not *see* the monster afore me, but my heart tells me that yer nowt but a bully. And all bullies are cowards.'

Zak trembled at the old woman's brave words.

'Yir pathetic, just like the rest of 'em!' Murdoch roared back. 'And if yir quite finished, Ah'll get on with my business of finding that little rat!'

'No, I'm not finished!' the old woman said sharply. 'I've one more thing to say.' She sat tall and put her hands on her knees. She pointed her useless eyes straight at the big man's greasy face and curled her lips. 'Before this morn is through . . . yer'll be where yer belong. Mark my words!'

'And where might that be, ye daft bat?'

The old woman momentarily forgot about the two boys hiding behind her. She stood up and delivered her final sentence. 'In the depths of hell . . . slave to Satan . . . doomed to eternity!'

Zak and Jack nudged up against one another, trying to

keep within the darkness of Mary Malkin's sack-like skirt. But Murdoch heard the scuffling sound from behind her.

'AH KNEW YE WERE LYING!' he screamed at her. He lashed out and knocked her sideways. She fell heavily onto the floor and cried out in shock. The two boys found themselves staring up at Murdoch's snarling features.

'*Two* rats!' the big man roared.

'Run . . .' Jack screamed.

Murdoch's legs were open just enough for Zak to spring straight through them. The startled figure brought the cleaver down ferociously towards Zak's head. But Zak was too quick. The cleaver missed him by inches and struck a different target . . . *Murdoch's own foot!* The big man screamed in pain as a jet of blood shot from the toe of his left boot.

Mary Malkin was already on her feet and cursing loudly. 'Leave 'em be! Leave 'em be! I can smell blood and there'll be more blood spilt afore long, Murdoch . . . and it'll all be yers. See if I'm right!'

Zak darted out of the door into the next room, Jack following and Murdoch limping after them. The big man cursed the old woman, cursed his bleeding foot; cursed everything and anyone he could think of.

Zak saw the machinery in front of him. He recognised it. *The torture instrument!*

A man stood by the machine, cutting into some bundles of wool. He cut the netting with a knife and removed the mats of woollen fibre ready to feed onto the spiked cylinders. Zak wondered if he was another scab.

Jack pushed him sharply from behind. 'Quick . . . through that far door, I know a good place to hide.'

Zak dashed past the huge carding machine.

Murdoch's voice threatened from behind. 'YE'LL NO GET AWAY FROM ME! AH'LL CATCH UP WI' YE . . . AND WHEN AH DO . . .'

The machine operator watched in awe as Zak sped past, closely followed by the limping Murdoch. 'What . . . what's . . . happening?'

'None of yir business!' Murdoch snapped at him. 'Just keep out of ma way . . . or else!'

The operator gawped at the cleaver held high in Murdoch's hand, its blade glistening with blood. He dived behind the spiked rollers and disappeared out of sight.

Zak found himself in the spinning room. Only one of the looms was working. A man and a woman stood in attendance. The woman looked anxious. 'Jack . . . it's not like you to be late. And who's your friend? You both look like you've seen a ghost. What's happened?'

Jack voice trembled as he spoke. 'It's Murdoch, Miss Heather. 'E's after me . . . us! 'E'll kill me if 'e catches me!'

The woman's face turned as white as candle wax. 'James! Get them into the bale store and put them down the hatch. QUICKLY!'

The man reacted instantly. 'Quick, lads! Through 'ere!'

He opened yet another door and ushered them through. The woman slammed the door after them, just as Murdoch stormed into the room.

Through in the next room, the man pushed the two boys into a corner, lifted a trapdoor and pointed down. 'Get down there and keep quiet. There's nowt but rats and spiders down there.'

Jack hesitated and held back. Zak held back with him; he didn't like rats and he hated spiders, but both were preferable to Murdoch's bloodstained cleaver! He pushed Jack down the rough wooden ladder and followed on behind. The door closed above them. They crouched in the darkness for the second time.

'Who's the woman?' Zak asked.

'Miss Heather! She's old man Greenland's daughter-in-law. She's really nice. Everybody likes 'er.'

'And the man . . . the one in the carding room?'

''E's one of the Greenland family. And the man up there . . .'e's a scab! 'Is name's John Wood and 'e's in debt. People are after 'im for money and that's why 'e works. And Murdoch will kill 'im as well if 'e gets the chance! 'E needs to 'ide as much as we do. But we shouldn't have come down 'ere.'

'Why not?'

'Like I said . . . it's all 'appening the same as last time. This is where 'e found me.'

Zak's heart skipped a beat as Murdoch's voice sounded from above.

'WHERE ARE THEY? THEY'RE IN HERE . . . AH CAN SMELL 'EM.'

'There's no one in here!' Miss Heather's voice retorted sharply. 'And even if there were . . . I wouldn't tell you! Now get out! You're drunk and you've no rights in here!'

'DON'T TALK TO ME ABOUT RIGHTS!' Murdoch boomed. 'YIR FATHER-IN-LAW HAS NO RIGHT TO CUT WAGES . . . BUT HE'S AS MEAN AS . . .'

'Don't blame him,' Miss Heather interrupted. 'It's you

that's the cause of all the unrest. Ever since the Master made you Overlooker, you've made everyone's lives miserable. No wonder the mill's in a mess. That's why the Master had to cut wages. And then you roused the strike . . . and good honest folk are suffering again. It's all down to you!'

'STOP YIR BLETHERIN' AND TELL ME WHERE THE BOYS ARE . . . OR YE'LL BE SORRY!'

Down below, Zak crouched next to Jack in the darkness, his heart beating to bursting point. Jack's body quivered beside him.

Miss Heather stood her ground. 'Those folk out there might be scared of you. But I'm not! I'll never tell you anything. Do your worst!'

A heavy slap sounded from above. And then a scream. Zak cringed, shivering with fright as something heavy crashed onto the boards over their heads. He guessed it was Miss Heather.

Jack's voice trembled like never before . . . *'This is where he'll try to kill me.'*

'But . . . but . . . how?' Zak stammered.

Miss Heather's groans sounded from above, followed by another voice. 'Leave 'er alone! She's a good woman. I'll tell yer where the boy is . . . but yer'll 'ave to fight me first!'

'It's all 'appening like it did before,' Jack sighed. 'That's John Wood. Murdoch will fight 'im and force 'im into giving us up.'

Sure enough, a scuffle sounded above the boards. The big man cursed and James Wood screamed. Another heavy thud sounded from above and Zak knew the battle was over.

'TELL ME WHERE HE IS OR AH'LL SLIT YER THROAT FROM EAR TO EAR!'

'Don't tell him,' Miss Heather's voice pleaded. 'Please . . . don't tell him!'

James Wood groaned pathetically. It was impossible to hear what he was saying. But a few seconds later, Zak watched in horror as the trapdoor lifted and light flooded in. The big, greasy head of Murdoch stared down into their hiding place, a mocking evil grin spreading across his face.

'SO THAT'S WHERE YE ARE, MA WEE BAIRNS!'

Zak heart raced as Murdoch started down the ladder. There was blood still dripping from his boot and the blade of the cleaver was stained crimson.

'I'm really sorry, Zak! I thought we might be able to change things . . . to do something . . .' Jack's voice sobbed. 'This is where it 'appens . . . where . . .'

'. . . Where he murders you!' Zak finished for him. He knelt up stiffly, clenched his fists by his sides, saw something on the floor, just behind the foot of the ladder.

'Well not this time, Jack,' Zak said through clenched teeth. 'Not if I can help it . . .'

22

Just Deserts

The dead rat lying behind the foot of the ladder had triggered something in Zak's mind. His memory flashed back to his nightmare . . . his encounter with Murdoch in the cellar . . . *the rat* . . . his attacker had screamed at the sight of it and fell backwards. And then Zak recalled the lesson at school . . . about dreams . . . Miss Woodward's words. *There are those who believe that dreams have a meaning . . .*

Maybe Zak's nightmare had a meaning – telling him of the big man's weakness – big furry rodents with long tails . . .

'COME HERE!'

As Murdoch reached the bottom of the ladder, Zak lunged forward and snatched up the rat's carcass. Murdoch shrieked as Zak thrust it towards his head. The rat's rotting corpse was foul smelling and sticky and it stuck to the big man's face.

'ARRGGGHHH . . .'

Murdoch dropped the cleaver, fell to his knees and clawed the dead animal away. Zak seized the opportunity, jumped onto the ladder and made his escape up through the trapdoor. Jack tried to follow, but Murdoch, angrier than ever, caught hold of his foot and pulled him back. As Zak emerged from the trapdoor, he turned back and saw Murdoch holding Jack's head in a headlock. He stared helplessly in horror as Jack screamed, Murdoch twisting his head until he fell silent. The big man threw his limp body to one side and started up the ladder.

Zak sprang towards the door leading back into the spinning room. Miss Heather was sat with her back leaning up against the wall. She was groaning, her eyes closed. She looked dazed. James Wood lay motionless on the floor and Zak thought he looked dead.

Murdoch was halfway out of the trapdoor. His whole face was screwed up into an expression of pure blood lust. 'AH DON'T KNOW WHO YE ARE BUT JUST WAIT 'TIL AH GET MA HANDS ON YE!'

Zak panicked. He backed up against the bailing room door and tried desperately to open it. At the same time, Murdoch straightened up and threw the cleaver. The bloodstained implement missed Zak by an inch, but tore through the edge of his ragged trousers and pinned him to the door.

Murdoch roared in delight. 'CAUGHT AT LAST! SAY YIR PRAYERS, LADDIE!'

Zak struggled like a trapped rabbit – his trousers were well and truly fast. Murdoch was out of the trapdoor and limping towards him, a strong smell of whisky fumes in his wake.

Zak pulled frantically at the cleaver. He grabbed the handle and pulled for all he was worth. It was embedded deep into the door and wouldn't budge.

'THAT'S FOR A MAN TO USE, LADDIE . . . NOT A WEE SCAB LIKE YOU! NOW WHO ARE YE?'

Zak pulled again with all his strength. This time the cleaver came free. He swung it round and caught Murdoch just below his right knee. The blade was sharp . . . very sharp. It sliced the big man's flesh and Murdoch's blood gushed again. He shrieked and fell back.

Zak dropped the bloodied instrument to the floor, wrenched the door open and bolted back through into the spinning room. He ran on past the noisy loom . . . the Spinning Jenny . . . and through into the carding room . . . *the torture chamber*.

The great rollers, covered in spikes, creaked and groaned as they rotated slowly. The room was empty . . . the operator gone . . . disappeared . . . no doubt fled from the marauding Murdoch.

As Zak stood there, wondering what to do next, the door flung open and Murdoch stood before him, the bloodstained cleaver back in his hand.

'NOWHERE TO HIDE THIS TIME, SON . . . AND NO ONE TO HELP YE!'

Zak gasped at Murdoch's appearance. His face was terrifying . . . the eyes piercing, the mouth twisted into a snarl and the blackened teeth clenched with frustration. The big man's body looked even bigger than before, bloated with anger, and his clothes were covered in dust and dirt. One of his trouser legs still dripped blood where the cleaver had cut into his knee, and the end of one of his boots was split open and stained crimson. He looked truly a monster, straight from a horror film!

Zak stood rigid . . . in his soldier boy stance . . . gripped with fear. There was nowhere to go . . . nowhere to hide. He was done for!

And then he remembered the St Christopher. Maybe he could buy some time . . . give himself another chance. He felt in the breast pocket of his jacket; the silver medallion was there. He took it out and held it in his outstretched hand.

'Will you take this and leave me alone?'

Murdoch held out a hand the size of a dinner plate. 'GIVE IT HERE!'

Zak did *not* want to move any closer to his enemy. He threw the medallion and Murdoch caught it easily. He stared at it . . . trying to work out what it was.

'NOWT BUT A FANCY CHARM . . .' He put it into his pocket and sneered. '. . . AND IT WON'T BUY YIR LIFE, LADDIE! YIR STILL DEAD MEAT!'

Zak thought of the engraved picture of St Christopher carrying his traveller on his broad shoulders. He sighed inwardly. Murdoch was right. It was nothing more than a worthless charm.

It was then that Zak spotted the tangle of string netting piled on the floor. Murdoch was standing on it, completely unaware. As quick as a flash, Zak dived to the floor and pulled hard on the netting. Murdoch's injured foot got caught up in it and as Zak pulled for all he was worth, the big man lost his balance and crashed to the floor. He landed heavily in a sitting position, jarring his broad back. Once again, he yelled in pain. As he sat spitting and cursing and trying to set his foot free, Zak saw a bigger pile of netting over in the corner. He rushed over, dragged it back and threw it over the startled man's head.

Murdoch's arms and legs flailed as he tried to cast the netting aside. He spat and cursed some more and finally began to laugh hysterically. 'IT'LL TAKE MORE THAN A FEW BITS OF STRING TO TRAP ME, LADDIE! AH'M TOO BIG A FISH TO FALL FOUL OF A WEE BIT OF NETTING! AND AS SOON AS AH'M FREE . . .'

But the big man was more snarled up than he thought. The more he tried to throw the mesh aside, the more he seemed to get tangled up in it. In desperation, he began chopping at the mesh with the cleaver.

Zak's heart sank. The strands broke easily beneath the sharp blade . . . the monster would soon be free to do his worst.

But Murdoch's chopping hand worked slowly; the big man was suffering from exertion, loss of blood and his brain was dulled by the intake of whisky. He snorted triumphantly as the sharp blade cut through the strings . . . until something tugged at his injured foot. He looked up in surprise. Zak followed his gaze and saw that one end of the tangle had caught on the spikes of the carding machine. The lowest of the huge metal rollers creaked and groaned and drew the tangled mass towards it.

Murdoch fell silent. He leaned forward and swung his cleaver at the strings around his foot. Some broke, but others were already tangled with other strings and the whole mass moved slowly on towards the lethal machine . . . dragging the big man's body with it.

'DAMN AND BLAST!' Murdoch cursed, swinging wildly with the cleaver.

Zak watched in awe as the huge turning drum drew its helpless victim ever closer. He stared with fascination as Murdoch's expression changed from seething anger to one of fear and panic. The big man's eyes bulged as his injured foot was pulled into the air and dragged onto the spiked surface of the lowest roller . . .

'SWITCH IT OFF! SWITCH IT OFF, WILL YE!' he screamed as he fell helplessly onto his back.

But Zak had no idea how to switch it off . . . and there was no one else around. He watched in frozen terror as the big man's body was reeled into the machine like a beaten fish.

'ARRGGHHH . . .'

Murdoch screamed a terrifying scream as his foot was drawn into the narrow gap between the lower roller and the one above it. There was a sickening crunching of bone and a splattering of blood as the big man's foot and lower leg were truly butchered. Murdoch fell back and screamed again as the netting took the whole of his lower body up into the machine.

Zak closed his eyes and put his hands over his ears.

The helpless Murdoch screamed his last as the whole of his lower body was crushed between two of the huge metal rollers. The machine finally jammed and ground to a halt. When Zak opened his eyes again, Murdoch's upper body was protruding from the machine, hanging upside down, the big bulbous face staring lifelessly up at the ceiling.

Murdoch was dead!

As Zak tried to come to terms with the horrific scene, the St

Christopher medallion dropped from the dead man's pocket and clinked onto the stone floor. Zak picked it up and hastily made his exit.

He ran the whole length of the building back to the bailing room . . . yearning for Jack still to be alive. He found Miss Heather leaning over Jack's broken body, crying hysterically.

'He's . . . he's dead, isn't he?' Zak asked, his bottom lip quivering.

'Yes.'

'And Murdoch did it!'

'Yes,' Miss Heather sobbed. 'He broke the poor boy's neck.'

Zak stared down at Jack in disbelief. *How could someone do something like that to someone so innocent . . . so . . . so harmless?*

'It's my fault!' Zak sighed.

Miss Heather looked up at him, dabbing her eyes with a lace handkerchief. 'Why do you blame yourself?'

'Because I came here to save him.'

Miss Heather frowned . . . a puzzled look in her eyes. 'I don't recognise you. Where are you from?'

'From another time,' Zak replied mysteriously. 'You would never understand.'

Miss Heather turned her attention back to Jack. She laid his head gently on the floor and rose to her feet. 'There's only one person to blame for all this and he's no doubt long gone by now.'

Zak said nothing and walked off. He went outside the mill building into the yard.

'It's over!' he said quietly to himself. 'I didn't save you, Jack, but at least Murdoch got his just deserts! If you can hear me, Jack, wherever you are, please don't blame me . . . I tried my best.'

He looked around, half expecting to see Jack's ghost standing there, ready to answer him . . . discuss what happened. But there was no one. Nothing! Just a deserted cobbled yard.

And then Jack realised that all the workers on the picket line had gone. The gates were shut . . . no one outside. Everything seemed different again.

In fact, Zak felt different . . . more like his old self again.

He held out his arms, looked down at his legs and saw he was wearing his own clothes. He scanned around the yard. It was as before . . . when he and Charlie had first visited it.

He was back in his own time.

He sighed a massive sigh of relief . . . and then felt intense sadness. *Jack was gone!*

He looked at his wrist. His watch was back: six o'clock in the morning, the time he had met up with Jack. It was like time had stopped . . . never passed. He looked at his watch again. The second hand was moving. Time was passing again.

He walked away from the old mill building, back along the quiet early-morning streets and finally turned into School Street. He couldn't even remember what day it was, he was so tired . . . and totally confused.

He walked towards number 21. No lights on – Mum and Dad were still asleep. *Thank goodness!*

He stared across at the playground. No one . . . empty. He sensed he wasn't going to see Jack any more. But perhaps at least he'd finally helped lay his ghost to rest.

He opened the passage door and clattered down the cobbles feeling a little cheerier. He wondered what Charlie would make of all this when he'd heard all that had happened. As for Mum and Dad, he knew exactly what they would say . . .

'Overactive imagination!'

Zak chuckled to himself, opened the palm of his hand and stared down at the gleaming silver St Christopher.

'Can I 'ave it back, please?'

Zak swung round. Jack was standing in the passage, face smiling and hand outstretched. His eyes were no longer wide with fright, his expression no longer sad and haunted. He had a look of calm . . . of contentment.

'Jack! I'm . . . so sorry!' Zak stuttered.

Jack took the medallion from him and slipped it in his trouser pocket. 'No need for yer to be sorry,' he said quietly. 'Yer stuck it out and faced up to 'im and Murdoch got what 'e deserved. 'E's no more and never will be.'

'But . . . but what about you?' Zak sighed.

Jack smiled. 'Yer did me proud . . . just like I knew yer would.'

'But how? He still killed you, didn't he?'

'That was down to fate, Zak . . . not yer! I was always going to be Murdoch's victim. But yer stopped 'im chopping my body up. And now I can rest.'

'What do you mean by "rest"?'

'Get yerself down to St Wilfrid's . . . to the churchyard and 'ave a look by the Devil's tree.'

Jack held out his hand. Zak shook it. It felt cold and tingly. 'Bye, Zak.'

'But . . . but . . . do you have to . . .'

But Jack had already gone. Faded right before Zak's eyes.

*

It was Saturday morning. Zak had bolted his breakfast down and made his way to St Wilfrid's church. He hadn't even been aware of the old church, but he found it easily up the other side of the river away from the mill.

He pushed the creaking wooden gate open and made his way into the churchyard. There were no signs of any trees anywhere. He made his way around the back of the church and finally saw a single oddly shaped tree with a bench beneath it. A small dark figure sat on the bench and as he approached, he saw that it was Mrs B. She was dressed all in black and was dabbing at her eyes with a handkerchief.

Zak walked up to her. 'Hi, Mrs B. Are you OK?'

She smiled up at him. 'I am now. I knew you'd sort things out.'

Zak noted that the old lady looked calm, content and the fear had gone from her eyes.

'What do you mean?'

She got up and led Zak over to a gravestone. A bunch of bright flowers lay in front of it. Zak moved closer and read the inscription:

IN MEMORY OF JACK CRADDOCK
DURING HIS SHORT LIFE HE SUFFERED
FOR OTHERS
NOW HE RESTS IN PEACE
1913–1925

Mrs B put her arm through Zak's and led him back to the

bench. She sat him down and sat beside him. 'He finally got what he always wanted, a church burial. Like it says on his stone, he's at rest. And close to the old yew tree, just where he would have wanted to be.'

'Is that what Jack called the Devil's tree?'

Mrs B looked at Zak with wonderment. 'Yes . . . my mother told me that Jack was always fascinated by it. They plant yew trees in churchyards to keep the Devil out, you see.'

Zak nodded. Now he finally understood.

Murdoch had killed young Jack again, but this time the big man had died in the mill and had never got the chance to get rid of Jack's body. And so, effectively, Zak had changed history and made it possible for Jack to have a church burial . . . and now his spirit was at rest.

'YESSS!' Zak said triumphantly to himself.

Mrs B looked at him in wonderment again. 'I don't know how you did it, but thank you, son. Thank you so much.'

Tears welled up in her eyes again and Zak left her and headed for home. He whistled to himself all the way back to School Street. He looked around at his surroundings and smiled. Nothing seemed gloomy any more. It was like a huge black cloud had lifted and let the sunshine in. He couldn't wait to tell Charlie . . . even he would have difficulty in believing all that had happened.

As Zak approached the boarded-up primary school, he glanced into the deserted playground, half expecting to see Jack standing there. But there was no one. And Zak wasn't surprised.

His heart was telling him that Scabbajack had gone for ever.

Epilogue

I recently became a full-time children's author and I went into a school today. I spoke in the assembly hall in front of the pupils and teachers. I told them about my childhood and how I'd moved into School Street when I was a boy. I told them about Jack – and what happened to him. I even told them about Murdoch's grisly end in the carding machine. I'm not sure the audience believed me. I'm sure they thought I'd made it all up.

One of the pupils, a young boy near the front, asked me if I was going to write a story about Jack . . . maybe turn it into a book. I told him I already had. I explained how it would be coming out soon and that I was really pleased with it.

The pupils got very excited. They asked me the title.

'Scabbajack,' I said. 'I hope you like it.'

They did like it. They said it sounded scary.

And then an older girl, sat near the back, asked me how she could become a writer. I asked her if she enjoyed writing. She said she did and that she writes all the time.

'Then you're already a writer,' I said.

She smiled proudly and I knew that I had made her day.

ZF

20:11:2025